I0741811

Behind the
Yellow Wallpaper

Behind the Yellow Wallpaper

edited by
Rose Yndigoyen

Also by New Lit Salon Press

I Voted for Biddy Schumacher: Mismatched Tales from the Mind of Brian Centrone
Retrospective by Michael Tice
Southern Gothic: New Tales of the South
Erotica by Brian Centrone

Behind the Yellow Wallpaper: New Tales of Madness

Published by New Lit Salon Press, 2014
© 2014 New Lit Salon Press

Edited by Rose Yndigoyen
Editor-in-Chief, Brian Centrone
Line Edited by Casey Ellis
Art by Loreal Prystaj
Art Direction and Design by luke kurtis

"Creeds" was previously published in *INK. A Journal of Creative Writing and Art*, SUNY/Westchester Community College, 2011.

New Lit Salon Press
Carmel, NY

Print ISBN 978-0-9885512-6-8
eBook ISBN 978-0-9885512-4-4

www.newlitsalonpress.com

Table of Contents

The Ideal Customer

Laura Hartenberger

Recently, I decided to tattoo my face. My entire face: lips, nostrils, eyelids, right up to my hairline.

When the idea first occurred to me, I was at work, creating a template. Most of my work was template-related. But nothing in particular prompted my decision. In general, things were going smoothly. My parents were still alive. I was getting regular promotions. I had friends, and a hamster. That morning, I'd gotten two new followers on Twitter.

The only explanation I can offer is that from time to time over the last year, I was completely overcome with uncontrollable feelings of rage. Rage against nothing and no one in particular. Almost instantly, I would become unable to think about anything except the anger that smothered every inch of my body: I couldn't eat or talk or move, except to beat up the floor, or tear a towel apart with my teeth, or rip limbs off a tree. After an hour or so, I'd feel fine again. I don't know where these rage episodes came from. There were no obvious triggers.

I was working as a Communications Associate for a marketing agency. My job was to prepare promotional materials—templates—for undefined products and services. The specific details of the products and services would be plugged in later. You didn't need to know what something was in order to create buzz around it. That day, I was drafting some preliminary taglines:

This mother's day, show your appreciation with our universally beloved and one-of-a-kind [blank].

Remarkably innovative and endlessly useful, now with updated technology: meet the new [blank].

You deserve more! This winter, treat yourself to a [face tattoo].

As soon as I made the decision, it felt as though a powerful spotlight had turned on overhead and I was lit up. Everything I was doing took on a sudden intensity. Every movement I made was an act of theatre. Every thought I had was original and good. It didn't matter that I couldn't see anything in the darkness around me.

For the rest of the afternoon, I could barely work. I just wanted to think about my tattoo. The content of the tattoo wasn't important. When I pictured my face tattoo, I imagined an abstract design with swirls and geometric shapes, maybe a couple words in subtle italics, something that worked off the lines and angles of my face. But I wasn't opposed to a landscape piece, or even a storyboard scene out of a movie. I was already planning to agree to whatever suggestions the tattoo artist made. It was important to me to be the ideal customer: flexible, accommodating, possibly the best tattoo customer of all time. Maybe I would just go into the parlor and give the artist free reign over my face. Thinking about doing that was so exciting that my knees started trembling and I had to remove my heels so they didn't clack audibly on the floor.

Looking around the office at my coworkers, I felt a thrill at the thought that none of them knew what I was about to do. "Going to get a face tattoo now," I tweeted before I logged off.

There was a parlor a few blocks away from the office. The guy had no visible reaction when I told him what I wanted. "I can do it right now," he said. "Are you ready?"

I didn't know exactly how the process worked—up to this point, I had no other tattoos.

"I'm ready." The artist sat me down in a suede armchair and pulled a stool over to sit in front of me. "Beautiful face," he said, adjusting the distance between us so his hands could reach my head comfortably.

I stared at him as he prepared his inks and machinery. His arms and neck were covered with tribal designs, and I noticed a small goat tattooed in the bald spot just above his left ear. The place smelled like metal and hamburger grease. His needle was like a tiny lawnmower grating up my face. I watched his eyes fill every one of my pores and was sure no one had ever paid this much attention to me. As he worked, I ran my tongue over my teeth and gums, feeling them vibrate. The pain was precisely the right amount of pain: just perfectly tolerable. It was entirely how I'd imagined getting a tattoo would be. The only thing I hadn't anticipated was the feeling of the bandages on my face afterwards: they were hot and they made me sweat, not just on my face, but all over my body. In the morning, I woke up so damp that at first I thought I'd wet the bed.

I took off the bandages and looked in the mirror. My face was so bloody and swollen that it was impossible to tell what it would ultimately look like. For a moment, I wished my face would stay forever at this

stage, clearly but ambiguously tattooed. I bent my head down in front of the hamster's cage. He approached me as usual, sniffing the air, but had no visible reaction to my face. Losing interest, he burrowed back under his wood chips. I felt the beginning of a rage—the stiffness in my elbows and jaw; the scream welling in my throat—but for the first time, instead of overpowering me, the rage just dissipated, and I was left standing there in front of the hamster cage, feeling nothing in particular.

I posted a picture of my bandaged face online and watched the responses appear:

OMG FOR REAL?

You crazy girl! I can't believe you actually did it!

Hahaha, looks painful!

Wow… and you had such a beautiful face.

Is that my name?

Leave Britney alone!

My mother posted, *Are you okay?* and left me four voicemails. I remembered begging her for years as a child to dye my hair—"It's too toxic," she'd say, or "You'll look crazy," and then, the rage when I discovered years later that she'd been quietly dying her own the whole time. I didn't call her back.

I took a couple of days off work—my face was covered in a sheen of pink goo and I was worried about infection. With more energy than I could remember ever having, I cleaned my entire apartment, even moving the fridge and stove to sweep underneath. I filed all my receipts and framed and hung photographs that I'd printed maybe two years ago. I'd known the tattoo would affect how I felt about myself, but I hadn't expected it to make me into a better person.

At work, my boss called me into her office. It was a fully transparent box in the center of the floor, designed for complete transparency, so anyone passing could see exactly what was happening in the most important room in the building at any moment. I put a hand on her wall, watching its skeletal print shrink and disappear.

"Doesn't it make you uncomfortable that anyone can see exactly what's going on in here?"

She ignored my question. "How are you doing?" she asked, focusing carefully on my eyes.

"I'm really great," I said. "Really wonderful."

"We're a little bit concerned about you," she replied. "Your changes," she made a window-washing motion in front of my face, "are a little bit worrisome, out of character. Some might say a little crazy." She laughed, lightly.

"There's no reason to be concerned," I said. "And this," I mimicked her hand gesture, "definitely won't affect my work here."

My boss cleared her throat and leaned back, nodding. "I am all for personal expression," she said, "but just so you know, this may affect your chances at future employment. It makes you into—well, a less-than-ideal employee."

"Less than ideal."

"I just wish that you'd come to talk to me about this first."

"To you?"

"Is there anything I can do," she leaned in again, "to offer you the *support* that you need?"

"Are you firing me?"

There was a very long pause. "No. Not at this point."

"Great." I moved toward the door, catching a glimpse of the reflection of my face in the glass. It was a blur of flesh and ink, and I couldn't make out the lines of the design, only my own human features. The impulse to put my fist through that spot in the glass came fast and hard. Before, I would've done it—punched through the wall with both fists, and maybe a boot—but this time, I took a deep breath and touched a hand to my face, which felt cool, and I imagined that the ink on it smelled like peppermint, and that it covered not just the skin on my face but also my hands and feet, the strongest, most delicate barrier between me and the world, and it was enough, not to calm me down completely, but to bring me, at least, to neutral.

Waiting for Jordan

Tracie Orsi

Julia Blake stands at the shoreline waiting for Jordan. He's been gone five months. Her eyes glisten as she watches ships drift over the Chesapeake Bay Bridge Tunnel on their way home to Portsmouth.

He'd been to Iraq before but this tour made her uneasy. Some of Jordan's friends came home in a box.

The morning before Jordan left, Julia knocked over the salt as she set his eggs on the table. She took a pinch and threw it over her left shoulder hoping it was the correct one.

"You don't have to go," Julia had told him. "You've put in your time, now you can go to school."

"We've been through this." It was their standard argument. Every married couple has one.

"The kids don't want you to go."

"The kids'll be fine."

Julia placed her hand on her belly. "You're a hero in their eyes. Stay home."

"Julia, you know I have no choice."

"I don't want you to go."

"I'll be home before you know it." Jordan kissed the tears from her eyes. Jordan sat down and dipped a piece of toast into the yolk. Yellow slime oozed across the plate like blood.

"They'll be here soon," Jordan said.

"I know. Please, don't go. Tell them you can't."

"Julia, it doesn't work that way. You know this." He shoved a forkful of egg into his mouth. The plate was gooey yellow, making Julia want to throw up.

"I'll be home soon, you'll see. The President said he's pulling us out. This is the last time. Then I'll go to school like I promised."

They were at a high school dance when they met. He was the most handsome boy she'd ever seen. He leaned against the wall surrounded by a group of pretty girls. Julia stood alone in a corner when he walked over to her. They made love that night in the back seat of his car and she woke up pregnant.

He dropped out of school and joined the military. This is all her fault.

Since Jordan's been gone, she dreams of the pretty girls by a reflection pool and feels giddy at the attention they give her.

In high school, they never looked at her.

Julia's not pretty in the normal sense, though Jordan tells her she's beautiful. She'll never be pretty like the girls at the dance.

In her dreams, Jordan stands at the far side of the pool watching her play with the girls. It's erotic in a way and she's not sure how she feels about touching herself in the morning.

Each dream is the same. Each night the vision of Jordan gets closer. Last night the girls noticed Jordan and they left Julia wading in the pool by herself.

At first, the dreams seemed funny to her, that with Jordan gone, she's having lesbian fantasies. She's attracted to the girls, they're all so young with big beautiful eyes and perfect bodies. She feels she's betraying Jordan in some strange way. Julia laughs when she tells the other wives about the dreams.

"Better watch out," she says. "I might fall in love with you."

"Maybe they're the Seventy Two Virgins of Paradise," says Janey Michaels.

"The what?" Julia asks.

"The Seventy Two Virgins promised to the suicide bombers if they die in the name of Allah."

"Did you know there are seventy two spaces from Start to Home on a Parcheesi board?" Betsy laughs. They play board games and drink wine while their husbands are away.

"Yeah," says Julia. "and seventy-two names for God."

"How do you know that?"

"I just know."

Julia puts the kids to bed and walks down to the beach. She's not afraid to leave them alone because she can see the house from where she stands. Besides, they're asleep. What could happen?

She digs her feet into the cool sand. The moonlight shimmers across the Chesapeake Bay. The sparkles on the water look like a thousand scattered pearls bouncing off the dark sheen. She imagines mermaids swimming beneath the surface, showing off their sea jewels.

Julia remembers her dream and steps into the water. It's warm and inviting. She looks back up the beach. Lights are on in most of the houses. She feels safe.

A breeze kicks up and Julia places her hands over her stomach. Jordan doesn't know. She didn't tell him when he left because she wasn't quite sure. She hasn't even told his mother. They call her Nanny Jo. Julia laughs at this. She misses her own mother who died when she was young.

The waves lap over her ankles. The water is calm—a small ripple folds onto the shore.

Endless *lap lap lap.* A beam of moonlight dances across the sand.

The water is almost to her knees. She sees movement further out and wonders, where's Jordan?

The girls from her dreams are just beyond her reach in the glittery pool. Stars dance across the water.

Warm water tickles her thighs and caresses her bottom. It feels so nice against her and she imagines Jordan's feathery touch. She throws back her head with a sigh and treads deeper into the Bay.

Easing into the water, her aching heart soothed as she touches her breasts. She forgets herself for the moment and imagines Jordan squeezing her nipples. She swallows water and gasps, sees the flickering lights from the bridge and turns back toward the beach. Her house seems far away.

She wipes the water from her eyes and swims back to shore.

Julia pulls herself up onto the beach and lays in the sand laughing. She thinks of the seventy-two virgins. Why would anyone want to die for such a ridiculous promise?

What happens after that? She asks the sky. They won't be virgins any more. Then, what?

Will she see Jordan in the sky one night as a shooting star? Will he be there to embrace her when she walks into the water one last time?

The waves wash over her feet. She sees the reflection of the moon on the water and hears the girls in her dream giggle. She pleads with them. Please send him home. Please let him come home.

She remembers the children and runs into the house. They sleep soundly. She lets the hot water from the shower rinse the sand from her tired body, climbs into bed and drags the covers over her head.

In the morning, Scooter's in the kitchen rubbing sleep from his eyes.

"Mommy, where's Daddy?"

"Come have some cereal." She puts him in his chair and pours a handful of Cheerios on a plate. "I'll make some eggs."

"Don't want eggs! Want Daddy!"

"I know, sweetheart. I know. He'll be home soon."

"No! He won't. Not coming home! I want him now!" The boy cries.

JJ walks in.

"I had a dream about Daddy last night."

"Oh, yeah? What was it about?"

"It doesn't matter."

"Here, come eat your eggs. Maddy, come here now. Stop kicking the table."

"Vicki Mason's dad was killed by a suicide bomber."

"Who told you that?"

"Teachers at school were talking about it. They said a little girl walked up to them. She had bombs strapped to her body."

"Maddy! Stop kicking the table! They shouldn't say things like that to scare children."

"Well, it's true." JJ throws his backpack on the floor. Julia rubs her stomach.

"JJ, get the juice from the fridge and come sit down."

"Mommy, I can't find baby Marly."

"Where did you leave her?"

"If she knew that, Mom, she'd know where to find her."

"Don't be fresh with me, JJ. I'll rap your head." Instead, she musses his hair and kisses his cheek.

He pulls away from her.

"Nanny Jo's coming for you today. You'll go to her house to play."

"Mommy, I want to stay with you. Daddy come home today."

"No, sweetheart. You go with Nanny Jo. Mommy's gonna clean the house for Daddy. Make it pretty for when he comes home."

"You think he'll be home today, Mom?"

"JJ, eat your eggs."

"More toast! More toast!"

"Mommy, I found baby Marly."

"That's good baby, that's real good."

The kids gone, Julia sits on a lounge chair on the back deck. The heat of the sun had already melted away the fog. The sun stands high in the sky and Julia steps into the yard to smell the rich sea in the air.

She sees a couple stroll down to the beach and thinks how happy she has been with Jordan.

"Mom? Mom!"

"What? What?"

"Mom! You were sleeping outside!"

"Mommy, are you alright?"

"Julia, darling, let's get you inside before the skeeters get ya."

"What time is it?"

"JJ, help your mother to bed. She's not feeling well. I'll put on tea."

JJ helps her out of the chair and to her bedroom. She sits on the edge of the bed and takes her son's hands.

"I'm so sorry, JJ."

"Don't worry, Mom. It's going to be okay."

"Just like your Daddy."

"He'll be home soon. I promise. Go to sleep. Nanny Jo's making us popcorn."

"For dinner?"

"No, silly Mom. After dinner."

Julia tosses all night. She's afraid to go to sleep for fear the virgin girls will drown her and take Jordan away.

Her heart races and she gets up to open the window. She smells the bay and the muddy scent of cracked oysters.

She places both hands on her belly. Julia is sure Nanny Jo knows about the baby though she hasn't told her. Mothers sense these things.

She splashes water on her face and climbs back into bed.

This night she doesn't dream of the virgins by the pool.

In her dream, the President salutes Jordan at the Naval Yard. Only Jordan doesn't salute back.

The American Flag drapes across a coffin. Jordan's best friends look fine in their dress uniforms but they're not smiling.

Madison climbs onto the bed.

"Mommy?"

"Wha-at?"

"Nanny Jo wants to know if you want waffles for breakfast."

"What time is it?"

"She says I can have mine with ice cream."

"Nanny Jo is not giving you ice cream for breakfast. Come here and give Mommy a kiss."

Madison giggles. Julia smells the sweet baby smell and folds herself out of bed.

The little girl follows her into the bathroom.

"Can I pee in peace, please?"

"When's Daddy coming home?"

"Soon, baby. Real soon."

"I miss Daddy." The girl cries.

"I miss him too, baby. We'll all have ice cream waffles for breakfast."

"You going to call the base?" Julia thinks Nanny Jo looks tired. She knows her mother-in-law feels the pain. She lost her husband to cancer when Jordan was twelve. A little older than JJ is now.

"You know how that goes."

"Right. You gotta pick yourself up, Julia. You can't let the children see you this way. You're exhausted."

Nanny Jo scoops the ice cream on the waffles and sets them down for the kids.

"I can't do this anymore," Julia says, as she runs into the bathroom and throws up.

"Jules?"

"I'm fine. Can you watch the kids today? I don't feel well."

"Does Jordan know?"

"I'll be fine."

Julia heads to the back yard and sits on the swing. A neighbor is sunbathing next door. The radio is on. The newscaster says that Obama just ordered more troops to Afghanistan. Damn it all. He said he'd pull the troops out of Iraq so he'd get elected.

Now he's sending them to Hell.

Please come home, Jordan. Please.

"It's one o'clock on this beautiful Sunday afternoon. Not a cloud in the sky ," says the radio announcer.

Julia walks into the house to put in a load of laundry. The dishes from breakfast sit in the drain board. Nanny Jo took the kids to the beach.

She walks down to the beach past the usual sunbathers. A few boys toss around a football, making diving catches into the water. Two old women are beachcombing.

Julia walks along the dune line toward the bridge. The sea oats sway in the breeze and the rustling sounds like whispers.

Sea gulls screech overhead.

She looks back from where she came, but the dunes hide her. The cars thwump thwump thwump overhead on the bridge.

A barge passes over the tunnel leaving port and out to sea. What will happen if Jordan doesn't come home? What will she do if the officers in uniform come to tell her?

Who will they send? Billy McDermott? Roddy? Mikey?

What a cruel thing to do. Send a guy's best friend to tell his wife.

Scavenging gulls circle above her, the glare across the water blinds her. Past the pylons a few fishing boats rock with the current.

She raises her dress over her knees and steps into the warm water. The Bay is calm today. Too calm. So smooth. The sun bounces off the water like diamonds.

The air is still, not like at night with a pleasant breeze. And the cars overhead, thwump, thwump, thwump.

Julia hears the giggles of little girls and looks to see. No one's there. The same giggles in her dreams. Two steps more and the water licks between her legs. Everything seems so far away. She calls out Jordan's name. He doesn't answer, of course. No one. Not even God can hear her under the bridge. It's choppy out past the pylons, rougher than near the shore.

She looks up at the sky. The current moves beneath her thighs. Though she feels heavy in her heart, her body is light.

"Come in, come in," the waves ripple with a twittering laughter.

"Jordan's here with us. He's in Paradise and he waits for you."

The water is now up to her belly. Can the baby feel it? Going to see your Daddy, now. She puts her hand down to assure her unborn.

Up to her shoulder, the water embraces her, the way Jordan once did. Her dress billows up around her and she looks like an angel floating through Heaven.

She can barely touch the bottom. She lays her head back so only her face can feel the warmth of the sun.

She feels herself moving toward Jordan. The sound of the cars muffled through the water in her ears.

She ignores the giggling girls and the old ladies yelling to her from the beach. She drowns out the warnings from the man fishing from his boat by the pylons. She listens to her heart beating, the blood rushing in her head like the waves flowing through a giant shell.

Drifting, floating with the Seventy Two Virgins in Paradise looking for Jordan.

"We'll take you to him," they whisper.

"Our baby, too?"

"Of course, your baby, too."

She hears her name called from a distance, through the water.

"Julia? Julia!"

Julia draws in a deep breath.

"Jordan?"

Pas de Deux

Gabriela Denise Frank

She was, in fact, the first girl I killed.

You might assume that I determined her future when I interviewed her, but that's over-reaching. Killing Kate Lee wasn't top of mind when we met—yet, of all the candidates, she shined. In the crease of her notebook she had written *Smile and be confident!* which, I admit, plucked my heartstrings. She was fragile and lean but also a fighter, qualities that piqued the latent mother in me.

She grinned and chirped nervously during the interview like the brightest student in class, the one afraid to raise her hand, though she knew she was right. Her timidity gave way to an eager display of acumen, a sin just south of vanity some might say. How the other children must have envied the way teachers warmed to her, brilliant and budding Kate Lee. The ingénue, the understudy, the humble apprentice—what coquettish hogwash. But first, her eyes.

Kate Lee was doe-eyed, which is to say that a great span of her face from cheek to brow was drawn wide with two windows of velvety brown iris. Her fluttering lids had the power to charm, or so I noticed as Marcel and I walked her around the office. Demure and wet, her glance communicated a virgin's hesitance, for that's how girls beguile trust in others, knowing as a serpent knows that we protect our young.

So thin she could barely keep warm in summer, she layered short tulipy skirts atop leggings with, of course, ballet flats. If she hadn't bleached her hair platinum blond, damaging it into a broken bob, she might have drawn it up in a bun to look like Olive Oyl on pointe. Skinned back in pins, the contrast of her white-blond locks and stormy eyebrows could be called striking. These details evoked pity in me; the poor soul hadn't found her sense of style yet.

When touring the mahogany-lined halls of the executive floor, Kate Lee made a point of standing in first position at our pauses, centering herself in pools of light. The nymphette was shy-thrilled when we asked about the dance experience she had listed on her resume. While unrelated to the clerk job, she knew it made her special. Like a lyric poet or painter, a dancer lives in a higher echelon than the rest of us who clod and galumph through life. Marcel, our department head, and I were intrigued.

Her references, all men, spoke highly of her gifts, claiming that Kate Lee had organized their chaotic lives and various crises, despite her age and inexperience. Her smile beamed in their memories, all of them taken in by Kate Lee's graceful subterfuge.

And so she came to join our family. At first, I was happy for her assistance, if not unnerved by her silent shadowing, as if my acolyte was not studying my actions but sizing me up. I passed down what I knew, reading through her first case logs, which were promising. Just past her three-month review, she rankled when I corrected her work where she purred for Marcel. Any upbraiding from him she took as education, whereas she bridled at my mere suggestions. I questioned my manner— *Would it offend Kate Lee if I pointed out a small misstep? It's only a matter of style. I'll mention it gently.*

In conversation, Kate Lee often lauded her father as an influence, a writer like she hoped to be. Doting and patient, he had clearly spoiled the girl. She described carefree days of growing up at his feet, cheering at football games of his alma mater where she later matriculated and camping together like ruffians in the Oregon forest while her brothers and mother stayed home. She would have been taken down a peg had she grown up under my father's rough-hewn hands.

Within six months, I despised her. Sometimes, she'd shoot sly sneers at me while the others weren't looking; I was the only one who saw it all. In meetings, she openly questioned my reasoning yet gained the team's support. *Kate Lee is young, but she really gets it*, they nodded in unison. Small and large, at every turn it was her against me. I fantasized about finding her former coworkers and classmates whom she had abused with her innocent stares, gaining the accolades that they might have captured had she never existed. It was pathetic to feel competitive with her, yet I sensed my toehold crumbling beneath my feet.

"Kate Lee," I called one morning. Just five feet away, she couldn't hear with her head phones on. "Kate Lee," I said again. Nothing. I rose from my chair and walked beside her. "Kate. Lee." I demanded louder, slower. She kept typing. I reached over to knock on her desk and she sat back, more irritated than startled, staring up at me dully, forcing me to be affable now that everyone observed our exchange. Later, I confirmed her ruse when she responded to Marcel's call through the very same head phones though the volume of his voice was shades lower than mine. Rising from her chair, she responded with an eager smile at the sound of his voice, her grin dissolving as it met me. That saucy bitch.

How I loathed facing her blank silence each morning, the way she snubbed my greetings while returning the grins and waves that came as she walked along the glass bank of the executive offices. As with all her slights, Marcel didn't notice. Her visage opened like a daisy when he or Arnold, one of the senior partners, called on her, a chorus of enthusiastic titters escaping her cherry red Lolita lips; at my questions, the flattest of two-word responses: "Not yet."

Each week, we tumbled further down, one circle to the next, hurtling toward an icy lake of spite. She scrambled to leave meetings that I organized and I ignored what little of her generic chattering I barely heard: a new apartment with her boyfriend, Scout; a vacation in Chicago; the TV shows and movies she liked. When I entered the room, her jaws clicked shut. What did I care? She could have her secrets.

With spring, changes emerged in the burgeoning weed, always pushing toward the sun no matter how many rocks I kicked in her path. First, the removal of her glittering chest piercing, which had always seemed pointless, as she had no bosom to accent. Then, the grow-out of her hair, a dingy clotted brown to replace the Courtney Love blonde. One wet April morning, she came to work with her hair down, reminding me of a drowned Yorkshire terrier—frizzy, bony and shivering. When she started straightening it and wearing tailored outfits and oversized hipster glasses circa 1970s secretary, I realized that she was trying to look more professional. She was trying to emulate me.

Early on, she had curried favor with Arnold and the other partners; with them and Marcel as allies, her star rose quickly. Without warning, Arnold gave one of my cases to Kate Lee as testing ground. His words, *It's time for her chance at the ropes*, spun turnstiles in my mind. I feigned agreement as she tapped her toes mid-air before scampering away to meet with him. Sensing that she hadn't allotted enough time for production, I suggested that she print copies the day before the submittal was due. Instead, she left at six that evening with the case unfinished, bidding goodbye to Marcel and Arnold but not me, as always.

I smirked when it fell apart. With imminent failure overhead the next morning, I offered help, but she refused. She wanted the glory for herself alone; let her demise be equally claimed. Instead, when she missed the deadline, her failure fell on my shoulders as her manager. Arnold's reproach sent her skittering to please him five times over; me, she blamed, both for not lending aid and for being in the position to offer it. Afterwards, Arnold directed us to see Robert, a consultant, at a meeting outside the office at an Italian café nearby.

"What we need to establish is trust—that goes both ways," Robert said, pausing to look at each of us squarely. With a thick helmet of white hair and an open, ruddy face, he served as our psychologist-at-large. Kate Lee's gaze went from reptile to victim. "Well, *I* don't have a problem with *her.*" A smile played on her lips. Older sister was in trouble; she only had to hold her resting pose and let the plot unfold.

"That's good. Let's try something. Would that be okay?" Robert was handling us carefully, a snake in one hand, a mongoose in the other. We consented reluctantly. "As her manager, would you support the career goals that Kate Lee listed today?" he asked me.

"Of course. There's nothing but opportunity for us all." I said smoothly. *See? I know how to play this game, too.*

"Kate Lee," he said deliberately, turning to face her, "do you recognize that we are here to help you achieve the success you want?"

"Yes," she whispered breathlessly, flashing a smile. She played him perfectly. From outside Robert's peripheral vision, her gaze slashed at me like Spanish steel.

"Then we can agree to make a plan and work together, right?" We each said yes, sheathing our fangs in smiles. When it was over, Robert sent her on ahead so that we could talk, bobbing in the wake of her enmity.

"She's at a stage of development where she's trying to separate from her mother," he explained when it was just the two of us. "You represent the force and control of an older female that she wants freedom from. She needs to differentiate herself and it's going to come across as disruptive. You have to be the adult here." I gave him a thin smile. He reached over and put a hand on my shoulder, "Come on now, I know you can do it." I nodded to please him, but deep down I knew that I wasn't the woman he believed I was.

When I returned upstairs, I found Kate Lee nattering away to Marcel and Arnold who were rolling with laughter near the atrium, something we no longer did as a team. At my presence, she returned to work, plugging in her headphones defiantly. Like a single parent of a teenage daughter, I had grown weary of our daily battles, which Marcel never acknowledged, the absent father of our department. An affable man, he preferred to ignore discipline problems until someone resigned.

I retired to the ladies room to splash water on my face, leaning forward to examine myself in the mirror, framed with that week's bouquet of orchids. *Enough of her*, I thought, disgusted; *what's happening to me?* The twenty years between me and Kate Lee had snuck up quietly. To men in their forties and fifties, I was still attractive, but the autumn of my life was approaching. My skin was less dewy, thinner than in my youth, the crepe paper lines deepening under my eyes. Further south, the swell of my breasts held a tenuous line between plump and sag while the upturn of my once-perky bottom threatened to disappear into the flat pancakes of a middle-aged rump. Kate Lee had everything before her—vitality, flexibility, sensuousness—if only she would let them blossom across the stage of her body.

I brushed my chestnut hair, which tickled the tops of my shoulder blades. It hadn't been this long since high school, a trend common among women my age. Thriving against the backdrop of powerful heroines in our youth, most of us cropped our hair into pixie cuts in college and graduated bobs in our thirties (thank you, Halle Berry and Jennifer Aniston.) In our forties, our attitudes were softening along with our once-taut bellies. Julianne Moore and Gwyneth Paltrow reminded us to embrace our femininity alongside our resilience and business acumen, to grow our hair like urban bohemians and pull it back in French twists before our napes became too wrinkled, requiring year-round turtlenecks a la Diane Keaton.

What a fool, Kate Lee, to starve her ballerina flesh in the august days of her womanhood. She must recoil at my voluptuous form, monstrous and undulating next to her orphan's build, hoping that my fate might never befall her. While she coveted my shiny mane, attempting to smooth her damaged remainders in a similar fashion, I could see her all the while chalking me up as a Gen-X washout, an out-of-touch has-been. She probably boasted to her friends what a loser I was, divorced and deservedly alone, at least in her eyes—how dare she!

I wasn't sure which was worse: feeling such blind anger towards someone, or the fact that I had allowed her, of all people, to provoke me. I was supposed to be the adult, as Robert said; instead I could feel

only adolescent outrage bubbling up in my throat. Everyone loved her. No one was willing to see what she was doing to me. A spiteful, wicked child was ruining my life. I was trapped. As I exited the bathroom, I slammed the door into the wall, punctuating my anger with a knob-sized hole in the drywall.

Writ large across the sky of my face, the fiery constellation of my resentment gave Kate Lee a start when I found her in the kitchen. On sight of me, she froze near the refrigerator. Her rigid posture reminded me of the pet hamsters I kept as a child, how they stood on hind legs trembling like little bears, sniffing the scent of my approach with twitching noses. Unbeknownst to us, the female we bought had four babies tucked quietly inside. After their birth, I watched them for hours with fascination. Naked and blind, they resembled tiny humans until their fur came. After their birth, I often caught their mother running erratic circles around the cage, stopping and starting as if a predator pursued her. The babies slept unaware, heaped into a corner under the straw.

Something went wrong one afternoon. I came to check on them as usual, lifting the screen to find the mother staring up at me with red beady eyes. Noticing tufts of fur in the corner, I gave the babies a gentle poke, but they didn't move. As I pushed my index finger into the fur again, the mother charged me. I pulled my hand away, feeling the graze of her half-inch incisors. As she skidded into the glass, she uncovered them: four bloody, decapitated babies. At the time, I couldn't imagine what would make her devour her young, but as I returned Kate Lee's glance across the kitchen, one animal to another, I understood. There was no controlling this uppity thing, no putting her back, no taming or schooling her. She had pushed her way into my world where she didn't belong and pushed me out at the same time. Neither of us was backing down.

Before she could escape, I walked towards her calmly, reaching out to touch the side of her face. Her skin was soft and smelled old-fashioned, like roses. We paused for a moment peaceably, Kate Lee growing malleable in my arms like Sleeping Beauty in a swoon. Her docile posture nearly charmed me until I saw a blink of betrayal in her eyes. Watching my intent become impulse, Kate Lee's pupils turned back inside her head like reels of fruit in a slot machine. They seized me, turned me over, took me down. Without warning, I slammed her head against the SubZero. Stunned, she didn't make a sound in protest, so I hit her again and again on the cold silver.

"Kate Lee, so sweet and brilliant!"

"Kate Lee, the clever ballet dancer!"

"Kate Lee, the shy introvert!"

"You shouldn't be so hard on her; you're the adult!"

It felt satisfying to give in, to deliver what she deserved, what so many before me had never achieved. All of those months she plotted for my job, warming whenever Arnold or Marcel entered the room, engendering herself with the male staff, chirping at their jokes, putting forth her ideas oh-so-skillfully under the guile of observations—after months of struggling against her cancerous will, small but intrepid, there was no end to what I could do by the power of my hands. Age and treachery defeat youth and beauty.

I smashed her lollipop head against the fridge ten times, but she slumped to the ground, stubborn in living. As I crawled on top of her, I wondered if that non-fat soy crap she drank made her frame porous like bird bones. That's exactly what she was: a singing canary on the outside and a squawking vulture beneath.

Feeling her warmth pour into me as I straddled her, I paused to straighten her head on the dark marble tile. I was going to have my way with her and that was that. We were on my time now. My fingertips began at her temples and worked down to her collar bones. "You don't need these, do you, sweetie?" I asked, pressing until they snapped, first the right, followed by the left.

Then her wrists, backwards—

Her fingers and toes—

The ulna and fibula, right and left, then humerus and radius, and finally, the bowl of her iliac crests, until, at quivering last, she was nothing but a bag of bones spoiled on the floor. Like a lioness who had brought down an elusive kill, I felt engorged with relief for a moment. But the deed wasn't done. Her heart wouldn't quit. She whinged, accusing me; it was this as much as her springtime radiance, the magic glow of a twenty-something girl whose power is just beginning to penetrate the world, that drove me mad. Somehow, just being alive, she diminished me. There wasn't room to share.

From the far reaches of the office, they were coming. We were surrounded by the cacophonous doom of confusion and deputizing—

posses and plans that would aim to save us both. Me, they could have, but not her. Her doe-eyes darted wildly beneath me, hoping for someone, some *man,* to come to her aid, but it was just us ladies, if only for a minute more.

"Where's your daddy to save you now?" I whispered through my teeth. She whimpered but didn't speak, her pupils trembling in their rheumy sockets, wiggled loose like a broken baby doll from Goodwill. She knew I was the last sight they'd ever see and for that, I almost liked her.

I stood, ruffling the skirt on her chicken bone thighs as I stepped behind the SubZero, rocking it back and forth like a mother pulling a mangled car off of her child. Marcel rounded the corner of the hallway, calling my name in slow motion. I held the fridge at the apex of the arc.

In those languid moments, crowned with a lustrous mane of hair and colors blazing, I was Wonder Woman; if I wanted to, I could save her. She looked up at me, her effusive will a tell-tale heart beneath the floor boards of my mind, thudding and thumping in the way that I could never get it to stop since we met, her rancor inside me like poison, inseparable, that pressing urge and her spite, her life-force draining mine—so I let go the weight. Her impertinence, her timidity, her dancer's composure, every bulimic facet of Kate Lee met in a puddle on the floor, her limbs quivering like a roach under my boot.

I felt Marcel's sweaty palms on my shoulders as I stared at her broken face, still beautiful despite its cracked facade. His stubby, callused fingers pushed me down next to her on the floor, like a criminal until the others came. My hands sticky with her suffering, I reached out to sweep a lock of hair from her face when I had the oddest thought: I swear, as she expired, she looked just like me.

Last Caress

Leah Chaffins

"I've been looking over your file. The only thing I don't understand is why?"

"Nothing is simple, nothing ever," she said as her arms pulled against the restraints making a loud clanking sound as the metal loops reached their limits. She looked across the table at the doctor. She knew before he had asked what he wanted; they all wanted the same thing. They were all dirty head-men in crisp suits. If he took off his jacket she would see the nearly-invisible outline of a white t-shirt under his button-up dress shirt. They were all the same. They asked the same questions, took the same notes, and smiled the same smiles.

"I bet you like this…seeing a woman tied up." She shook her hair back over her shoulders and looked seductively at the man. His head angled softly and she saw he looked at her more intensely just as the previous doctors had when first they talked. They all seemed surprised that she spoke so proper, with a vocabulary that marked her intelligence. It was as if her throaty and refined voice usurped their preconceived idea of how she would speak, as if they expected her to speak coarsely, as if the jumpsuit determined her word choice and mannerisms.

She really wanted to scratch her face, and her inability to move her legs was causing her lower back to ache. Her calm face belied her internal grimace at the stale scent of the institution. It smelled like generic pine cleaner and sweaty people. She stared intently at the doctor, occasionally hooding her eyes, and biting at her bottom lip.

"You will find that I am quite immune to your games, Ms. O'Conner. Now, please, tell me why?" The man pushed his glasses back up the bridge of his nose. She could see the glasses needed adjustment, and could tell he kept procrastinating the fix. He had a new passion. She was sure his curiosity gnawed at him hungrily. She could tell he felt highly doubtful that she would answer his questions. The list of respected psychiatrists that had visited before him was substantial; she had refused to answer their questions so odds were high she wouldn't answer his. It

was obvious to her he wasn't going to let that stop him from trying. "Just start at the beginning," he said.

The woman chuckled. "Many have asked, but I like you. I think that if I ever get out of this quagmire, I would enjoy furthering our acquaintance." The woman looked at the man with mischievous eyes. She leaned against the chair, stretching her back. He was looking at her breasts which were pushed out due to the chains locking her hands down against the chair and the way she held her shoulders. She smiled at him smugly when his eyes grew large as he realized he had been caught. She waited until he looked away, down at the floor, and shifted unconsciously in his seat.

"My reason is one last caress. Une dernière caresse. Do you have any children?"

"That's a personal question," he said.

"These questions you are asking me are personal questions," she said. Her voice was soft in its quickness.

"No. I do not have children," he said clearing his throat.

"Would you like to have a baby? With me?" she said. Her smile was sinister.

The man again shifted uncomfortably in his chair. She noticed that he had turned a little pink over the course of the last few minutes. She rolled her eyes as she thought of the predictability of these encounters. The sameness was tedious, but it did break up the monotony of sitting on the stained mattress of her cell. She thought of herself as catlike as she toyed with the doctors. They had all been male so far. She thought about how it would not be as predictable if a woman doctor came. A woman would not fall for her games, but the men who came, they were toys; toys sent to break her monotony.

"Here's what I know, Doctor—?"

"Jamison. Dr. Jamison," he said

"I know that my case is the big break you are hoping for. I am probably a book deal, and your career is flagging; you're graying at the temple; time has become your enemy. You've convinced yourself that if you can figure me out, then you will become renowned in your field. You started out wanting to be in the big leagues, making the big money, working the high profile patients, and life wouldn't cut you a break. I come along, and you think, 'This is it. This is my shot.'" She paused. "I can make that happen."

The sound of her voice saying those words sounded rehearsed inside her head. It would all have felt very déjà vu-like if she would have let it.

She watched as the man sat taller. This was the point where they all sat taller, more pronounced, more confident.

"You know, the camera in here is broken. I am not supposed to know that, but I do," she paused for dramatic effect. "I want a cigarette, and a kiss - a real kiss. Kiss me like you want to know my secrets. *Embrasse-moi comme un amant.*"

"That is not going to happen. I would be stupid to let you have a hand to hold a cigarette, and I won't be kissing you. I like my tongue attached to my mouth." He sounded sure, but she knew he was on the fence.

"Ah, and I thought you wanted to talk," she said. She dangled her story before him, luring him, begging him to play with her. She knew he wanted in her head to know her secrets in a bad way and yet he answered just as his predecessors had. All psychiatrists had, at some point, had the chance to interview male serial killers, but women serial killers were rare. The opportunity to interview a woman like her was possibly a once in a lifetime chance. Everyone wanted to know why she was a killer. Was it one incident or repeated childhood traumas that made her a killing machine? She knew she was a beautiful anomaly. Whoever she opened up to, or revealed herself to, would write the story making that doctor's career and possibly even lots of money. She knew she was as good as gold to these men. Only one would get her story and they would play her game by her rules.

"You hold the cigarette for me, and when you kiss me, only my tongue will leave my mouth. Yours can stay put."

"I don't think so. I like my job," he said the words spoken to her so many times before.

"No problem. Soon, another doctor will come along—every week or so a different one tries. Eventually one will do what I want…and he will get the golden ticket." She rolled her head back and looked up at the ceiling, dismissing the doctor with indifference. "One last caress, what does that mean?" he said. She laughed at the man, who was tenacious by nature, as he tried again.

The woman continued to stare indifferently at the ceiling, saying nothing. The clock, which sat inside a wire cage, ticked away at the silence. It hung on the wall behind her so she had no idea how long he sat waiting. Finally, she heard his chair push back and shortly after the door buzzer went off, and she heard the click of the door locking as it slammed shut, echoing through the room.

In the silence that followed she sat counting the tick-ticking of the relentless clock. 382, 384, 385. No longer distracted by the doctor's presence, she would occasionally, from another part of the facility, hear screaming or the slamming of a cell door. 407, 408, 409. Again, she heard the buzzer and the opening of the door. When she looked over, to her surprise the doctor was lighting a cigarette.

He pulled his chair in front of hers and sat down. He lit the cigarette, hesitating for a moment before he held it to her mouth. She too hesitated for a moment before inhaling deeply, savoring the richness of the burning leaf. She closed her eyes, and exhaled slowly. With her eyes still closed, she licked her lips tasting the coolness of menthol. He continued to hold the cigarette for her as she slowly smoked it to the butt. Each drag was slow and treasured. She savored not only the taste of the cigarette, but also the win. Finally, she exhaled, "Now, kiss me."

She felt him lean in and placed his mouth over hers. She ignored the fact he kissed like a dead fish as she ran her tongue over his teeth. The kiss was her trophy and so she loved it intensely. When he started to pull back, she softly yet firmly bit his lower lip just to remind him that this was her game. She knew he understood when he opened his eyes and found her staring right into his eyes. He rubbed his lip nervously as if the ethicalness of it all left a feeling, a stain, where she had kissed him. He was so easy for her to read. With every move, gesture, he belied his motives, thoughts and feelings.

He said, "Your turn." He set a digital voice recorder on the table that had originally been between them, pressing the controls to begin their conversation.

"One question first, will you put the kiss in your book? Or shall it remain our little secret?"

The doctor turned red at her question, and fiddled with the controls of the machine, restarting it. She sat staring at him long enough to see impatience creep into his face.

Almost there.

She sat a little longer until his eyes began darting between the door and the now crumpled cigarette butt his fingers twisted and fidgeted with. She knew he was questioning whether she was going to uphold her end of the bargain. She sighed, and smiled, "Golden ticket time."

Her sophisticated, husky voice had changed into a small town

Midwestern drawl. Her shoulders pulled forward and her breasts were no longer pushed up and out begging his attention. Her eyes no longer held the deadly glint. It was as if she blinked her eyes and became someone else.

"The first one was in Oklahoma. I picked him up at an all-night diner off Interstate 44. I was already four months pregnant, and needed some cash. It wasn't new to me; I turned tricks when my cash ran short. We got in his truck 'cause he said he knew of a place not far from town that would fit our needs." The woman blushed and looked down at the grey grout that lined the white tiles of the floor.

"On the ride out of the city he stuck in a home-burned CD and lit a blunt. Being pregnant, I told him no thanks when he offered me a hit. I had to look out for the little one in me. I patted my belly softly and smiled. I was going to make a good life for me and my baby. I must have imagined a million times about holding her in my arms. She and I, well, I planned us a really good life. I hadn't believed in anything in a long time, but she was there inside me and I knew I could believe in her. I dreamed of our life together.

He drove us out to the middle of nowhere, real boonies, and pulled over on an old dirt road. He sat smoking the weed and watching me as I worked at getting my jeans off in the small cab. He had been all soft and sweet up to this point, but once we began having sex that all changed. He was rough, kept saying he wanted his money's worth. I told him he was hurting me, but he didn't care. He said, "Whores don't hurt.

"After that he pushed into me harder. It seemed he drove as hard as he could," the woman said. She began crying and her fingers wrapped around the loops of her leg shackles as she realized she was unable to wipe her tears. She hunched forward a little as she remembered how it felt like as he was pushing into her stomach and how badly it had hurt. Her hair fell from behind her shoulders and hid her red face.

"Finally, the pain was just too much and I began screaming, which made that bastard laugh. I felt something rip inside me, and a lot of wetness coming from my girl parts. I knew he had killed the baby inside me.

"I really wanted my baby. I already loved her so much. I'd find a way to make a good life for us. She was gonna be my new beginning." Her face never changed, she just stared at the doctor to see how her story affected him. He sat writing notes on his notepad, smiling.

"It's all real clear. He jumped off me, his maleness dripping with bloody water. He started screaming at me, 'What the fuck? Oh my god, you nasty bitch. What the fuck is that?'

"I looked down and there was my dead baby on the truck seat. The stereo blared The Misfits "Last Caress." Like I said, I was only four months, and she wasn't really developed, but I could tell what it was. I mean, like, it had come out of me and, well, my heart knew."

She patted her chest, and continued, "I was shocked dumb; I mean, I had never heard of a spontaneous abortion. I ran one finger down her slick little cheek and watched my tears hit her filmy eyes and run off her nose before splashing away to nothing."

"He reached down and tossed my baby out the truck door like she was a piece of trash. I can still see the red dust scatter around her as she hit the ground. He looked out the open door and stared at her as if she were the monstrosity. 'Holy fuck,' he said and began shaking his head.

"I sat up, grabbing my jeans. He had come around to the other door, driver's side, and climbed back in. All I could think was that he killed my baby. I looked down and saw a pen. You know the kind, plain ol' black stick pen."

The woman stopped talking and looked over at the doctor. He was still smiling and writing on his notepad feverishly with a pen she recognized as a Montblanc. Finally, he looked up, "That's horrible. Go on." She marked his insincerity.

"So, I grabbed the pen. It was like all the anger I had ever felt filled my body. I didn't even feel mad anymore. I passed regular anger into a whiteness that was pure anger. I didn't feel the cold and I didn't feel hurt anymore. I only felt the white anger. I grabbed the pen and shanked him as hard as I could in his neck," she said. Her legs pulled against the restraints as she imagined the doctor with a pen stuck in his neck and she became acutely aware of her wetness.

She shook her head and continued, "He screamed and pulled back. The pen was still in his neck. Bloody bubbles were coming out from around where the pen had gone in. I pulled it out and swung it again. It went deeper on the other side. Blood was spurting from him. I climbed on top of him and grabbed his hair, pulling his head back. The blood spurted up hitting the roof of the pickup cab, and fell back down like ruby teardrops. The Misfits were still singing and I began to hum along with the music. He was growing weak real quick like. I was still on top of him, feeling the warm rain fall on my face. I ran my hands over my cheeks and inhaled the thick scent of copper. Leaning forward, drunk with rage-like desperation, I licked his cheek, tasting my baby's vengeance.

"Blood for blood, you know.

"When he quit moving and I was sure he was dead, I jumped out of the truck and grabbed my baby off the dirt and ran through the trees that lined the road. I ran a long time. There were moments when I was sure his spirit was chasing me. I ran from his ghost and from what I had done. I ran until I calmed down enough to realize my stomach was hurting really bad. I could feel blood running down my thighs. By the time I came to a wide creek, I was nearly doubled over. I walked into the water and washed his blood off me and my baby girl. The current was quick and I stood there, my stomach and back gratefully numbed by the cold pushing water.

"I held her in my palm and put her limp body up to my breast. My nipple was too big for her small grey lips to get around, but I tried anyways. I willed her to breath; I prayed to suddenly feel her suckling life into her, but deep down I knew it was hopeless. I sang to her softly. This time, instead of lowering her into her crib as I did in my fantasies, I lowered my hands to the chilled water and let the current carry my baby away.

"I tried to sleep by the creek, but I had begun hurting so badly and I kept seeing my baby and hearing The Misfits. I saw his face, the way he looked as he drove into me… and then the way he looked as the life left his eyes. I liked it. I liked it a lot," She looked over at the doctor.

"I felt infused with power, merciless and divine. Of course I killed again. That's why I am here. They didn't put that death on me until I told them about the others. You've got my file. You know this." She looked over at the man and he was looking at her. Her voice had changed back to sophisticated and her eyes were alive, pulsing with that ever-present predatorily gleam.

"Well, that does it for today. I will come back as I have more questions," the doctor said reaching for the voice recorder.

The woman had enjoyed her visit with the doctor. Her nipples hardened as she thought about his future visits, and there would be more; her story had but just begun. She felt a familiar yearning where he was concerned just as she had with the men she had killed after the first one back in Oklahoma.

"You and me, Doc, we're gonna have a baby. I've decided. You know, I will get out, or get loose one day. When I do, I will find you. You will wake up in middle of the night with my arms around you, humming softly in your ear." Again she paused. "I will let her refer to you as Daddy."

She watched the doctor redden at the idea of having sex with her and then she watched the color drain from his face as he realized what that meant.

"I'll rape you easy before I kill you, darling," she said leaning back in the chair and spreading her legs as wide as the restraints would allow.

"You're crazy," the psychiatrist gathered his notes and voice recorder as quickly as possible so he could make for the door.

She laughed softly. "They didn't put me in a straitjacket for nothing." She looked down at the restraint pants she was wearing, and the loops hanging off them that locked her legs to the chair.

She pouted as she regretted not having bitten off his lower lip.

The doctor was buzzed through the door, and slammed it quickly behind him. Once again, she laughed softly. "Sweet dreams."

The Good Fairy

Colleen Quinn

It was a harder sell than Patty had anticipated. Rob blinked furiously and said, "I didn't know you wanted to have a baby."

Some women might have been puzzled and hurt, but Patty found Rob's recalcitrance fortifying. In a funny kind of way, his lack of enthusiasm made her realize how badly she wanted to get pregnant.

"Rob, really! Why wouldn't I want a baby? We're not getting any younger, you know."

She took his silence for acquiescence, confident that she was right. She was thirty-eight, Rob was forty, although he didn't look it, a few silver hairs at his black temples the only sign. What if they had trouble conceiving? If they waited any longer, there wouldn't be any time to do anything about it, so she simply went ahead. She went off the pill, stopped drinking, monitored her diet even more painstakingly than usual, and transformed her husband's study into a small, attractive bedroom.

"Why do we have to do this now?" Rob complained. "You're not actually pregnant. Where am I supposed to work?"

"You have a laptop, silly, you can work anywhere. The baby can't sleep on the fire escape."

Anyway, the room looked much better painted a nice sunny yellow. That heavy red made the room look tiny and it took just forever to cover it up. Five coats! Up and down the aluminum ladder, all by herself, naturally, as Rob worked in the theater offices now that he didn't have an office at home. Patty played classical music on the radio to help the baby's brain develop and massaged her lower back. She thought, if I were really pregnant, I bet I would be exhausted right now. But she wasn't, so she stayed up past midnight packing up all those dusty theater posters and shopping online, barely concerned when Rob had not come home by the time she went to bed. He had cast his latest play and started rehearsals, which nearly always ran late.

He looked at the boxes as they started to arrive, expressing enough interest to actually open one and find twelve dozen pairs of tiny white socks.

"I'm sure I read in Dr. Sears that babies come with feet," Patty said defensively.

"That's 144 socks. Do you want a baby or a centipede?"

She stared at him blankly.

"Patricia, my love, I think you should relax."

"You always think I should relax," she smiled.

"And I'm always right. I read somewhere that some cultures consider it bad luck to buy gifts for a baby before it arrives."

Patty had been told to relax all her life. She could remember practicing the piano, playing the same piece over and over, never really getting it right, and her mother would sing out from the kitchen, "Patty, you're trying too hard."

What an awful thing to tell a child! She would never, ever say that to her baby.

There was something about the enforced idleness of a pedicure that calmed her and she tried to visit the salon on Flatbush Avenue at least once a week. She had her fingers and toes done, closing her eyes as the massage chair worked her lumbar region and the oldies station played Smokey Robinson and the rain came down. When the nice Filipina woman wrapped her toes in tissue paper and slipped on some ridiculous flip-flops, she hobbled over to the drying station by the big front window.

She thought the couple looked familiar. They came out of the sushi restaurant next door and laughed. Clearly, they had been in there a long time—Patty imagined massive slabs of polished wood loaded with sashimi and innumerable tiny cups of sake—for they had no idea it had started to rain so hard. Patty didn't eat sushi any more; she had heard the high mercury level in tuna was bad for the baby.

They huddled under the awning of the nail salon, so close Patty was just inches away and could hear their conversation. She recognized the woman, with a boyish figure and that dramatic flame-red hair you can't get out of a bottle. She was an actress, yes, that was it, and Rob had cast her in one of his plays. Her name was Fiona Lynch and the smiling man cradling her face in his hands as they laughed at the pouring rain was Patty's husband.

Patty held her hands and feet perfectly still under the blow-dryers, sure that she must be seen. How could they be so close and not see her? Couldn't they feel the waves of her rage washing over them? The fake

orchid on the windowsill provided no cover at all.

She heard every word he said. "I'll tell her tonight."

Then he kissed her and his eyes flicked downward to Fiona's trim little belly and Patty knew everything.

He arrived late and a little drunk. That was more obvious now that she wasn't drinking herself.

"I already know," she announced without a hello.

"Oh?"

His casual air enraged her. "Fiona Lynch is having your baby."

"Jesus, you *did* already know. I'm so sorry, Patricia. We didn't mean for this to happen."

She stared at him, eyes huge and angry. "Do you understand what you've done?"

"Look, I'll go," he offered, as if that wasn't all he wanted to do in the first place. "We can talk about it later, I'll only say something stupid if I stay."

And off he went, probably relieved, to his new girlfriend—such a younger-sounding word than wife—and their new baby and new life and Patty was left to consider her options. When she had spotted him with Fiona, Rob's smile had been incandescent. He never looked at Patty like that and she knew he would not be back.

She was not pregnant and would not be so any time soon. Obviously, Rob didn't have any fertility problems so those were hers alone. Could she date? Could she find someone to have a baby with and do it before she got much older? She thought about it, tried to come up with a description of her new perfect man and she couldn't think of anybody she could even bear to have dinner with.

She did not go into work. She didn't answer the phone or check her email. A financial analyst, she usually lived to monitor financial markets all over the world but the Hang Seng was just going to have to live without her while she researched adoptions. Domestic or foreign—look at all the cultures that just threw little girls away!—it would take years and years, a mountain of paperwork and an equally sized mountain of money. A lot of places thought she was already too old, a lot more didn't like single parents. She stayed in the baby's room, ensconced in the deeply upholstered rocking chair she had bought from Crate & Barrel to sit in while she breastfed.

It really was very pleasant here. Patty lived in a duplex apartment in a brownstone on St. John's Place in Brooklyn. The front rooms faced the street and the back rooms faced the rear of other apartments on Sterling Place. In fact, when the family moved in across the way, she called them the Sterling family. Her baby's room looked directly into the Sterling baby's room and her kitchen looked directly into the Sterling kitchen. Sterling Mother looked like she was going to deliver any day. Patty was sure that a woman so very pregnant shouldn't be moving boxes at all, not that they had a lot of them. She decided to keep her eye on Sterling Father; you would think all those tattoos might frighten a child.

She was surprised at how long it took them to set up the crib. Patty had done hers in under an hour and she did it by herself. These two squabbled all afternoon, dropping the slats and consistently mislaying the screwdriver. Don't forget! You have to check the screws every couple of months to make sure they're still tight. They won't check; Patty knew they wouldn't check. It took them forty-five minutes just to wrestle a crib sheet onto the little mattress and then they both had to sit down. Sterling Father had a beer—from the bottle, no glass, maybe they hadn't unpacked them yet—and Patty was appalled to see Sterling Mother take a sip.

It was like theater. She was a floor above the Sterling family and she didn't think they could see her. Still, she kept her lights off and only used her binoculars when something really good was going on, afraid the reflection off the lenses might give her away.

She took a leave of absence from work, supposedly to deal with Rob's departure, but really because she didn't want to miss it when the Sterlings went to the hospital or when they came back with a baby. She left the apartment for a few hours only when Rob returned to move out. She hoped he noticed the shiny padlock she had installed on the door of the baby's room. It would be like him to think himself entitled to the baby's things just because he was going to have one. Well, he wasn't going to get them, not one ducky or diaper would he take out of here. While he was there, she walked around the block, looking at the Sterling Family's building from the other side.

If Patty had a baby, she would be up at all hours. She had read in one of her books that newborns had to be fed every two hours around the clock. This didn't seem possible to her—who could keep up with that?—but she felt justified in staying up all night in the baby's room. She was glad she did for the Sterlings' lights flicked on at three in the morning and she got to watch as panicked Sterling Father ran around from room to room. She swore she could read his lips through her binoculars, "Have you seen the car keys?" Really, such careless people!

They were back the next day. It was shocking how hospitals threw you out as soon as they could. She watched as people came and went, bringing food and gifts. It was spring and if she kept her window open and the Sterlings did too, she could hear the baby cry. She was often at her post, watching, before either Sterling parent shuffled in to tend him. She didn't think they were breastfeeding; the baby drank from a bottle no matter who fed him. She had a clear view of the changing table so she was able to confirm that the baby was a boy. "Get out of the way," she muttered to Sterling Mother as she craned her neck to see.

Would the Sterlings think she was crazy if she gave them a gift? She didn't know how she would explain herself face to face, but she really thought she should give them something. The solution came to her in the middle of the night. Goodness, it had been staring her in the face! Her apartment had a fire escape that led down to the scruffy yards between the buildings and the Sterlings had one just like it. She just had to get over the rickety fence that separated them and then she could climb their fire escape and leave a little something on their kitchen windowsill. They would think fairies had brought it! She chose a little silver cup from Tiffany still in its sky-blue box. She had meant to get it engraved as soon as she could think of a name for her baby, but she hadn't decided on one yet. Tie it up with a sweet white bow and she was all set.

Patty waited for Sterling Father to leave for work. He carried one of those bike messenger bags but he was clearly not a bike messenger. Maybe a designer or artist of some kind? He left late—it was 9:30 before he was out the door—the way she imagined most artists did. Rob was almost never fit to go anywhere before ten.

Then she waited for the morning nap. Sterling Mother slipped the baby out of his sling carrier and into his crib. She backed away silently, clearly headed for her own bed, judging by her stagger and frumpy sweatpants. Patty leaped into action, unsure how much time she would have. By her observations, sometimes the baby's morning nap was two hours, but sometimes it was only twenty minutes. She scrambled down that fire escape quick as a monkey, her little package in a shoulder bag. It was easy to get over the fence, fueled by adrenaline as she was, and no effort at all to jump for the lowest rung of the Sterlings' fire escape. She was lucky to be tall and she ignored the flakes of paint and rust fluttering into her face.

She crouched outside the Sterlings' kitchen window and slid the screen open quickly and quietly. She had intended to just leave the little package there and climb back down, but once she was there, she had to look around. How could she resist? She felt like she knew the Sterlings so well. The kitchen was even messier than it seemed from across the way. Breakfast cereal bowls filled the sink, an empty wine bottle rested by the full trashcan, and the floor could certainly use a good sweeping. She couldn't leave her gift there; they might not find it for weeks.

She tiptoed out of the kitchen, her heart beating its way up her throat. She got a very nasty turn when she passed a mirror. She didn't recognize herself at first and no wonder, looking so wild! Hairbrushes, clean clothes, they just hadn't seemed very important recently. Patty took just a peek into the bedroom to check on Sterling Mother, passed out on her back like a dead woman, arms and legs flung over the edges of the unmade bed, and then, oh so quietly, she slipped into the baby's room.

He was an angel, an absolute angel, a true redhead with long eyelashes the color of sunlight. She didn't know how he came by such good looks, his parents were quite plain, drab even. Fiona Lynch had red hair so Rob could have a baby like this and probably would, another stroke of luck for a man who had done nothing at all to deserve it. It was so unfair, Patty could feel the sour acid in her stomach gurgle and revolt. The baby also slept with his arms and legs splayed, like a parachutist coming in for a landing. The poor dears, they'll never know they sleep in the same position. Patty clapped a hand over her mouth as if she had spoken the thought aloud, for all at once she knew she would not be dropping off a gift.

What luck! The Sterlings had the same baby sling she did. A true believer in market research, Patty had watched the instructional video online and knew exactly how to loop it over her body. She found a little cap to cover his beautiful hair and eased him into the sling. He snuggled comfortably, curled up like he was back in the womb. Patty smiled and thought—I could do this. I could be really good at this.

On her way out, she noticed a stack of cards from the baby shower. She flicked one open and learned that the baby's name was Ronan. She turned the lock on the front door as quietly as she could and took the stairs slowly, protecting the baby's head with one hand. Out on the street, she was terrified. What if she ran into someone who knew the Sterlings? What could she possibly say? But Ronan was so small, it was hard to see him over the sides of the sling and Patty just had to go around the block. I don't look any different from anyone else, Patty realized, I look like someone's mother, and she strolled back home unhindered.

The baby was just starting to stir when she got home. She laid him out in the crib, so clean and fresh, and ran to close the windows. If she could hear Ronan when he was with the Sterlings, they might be able to hear him from her apartment and she wouldn't put them through that. It would be cruel.

The Safety Pin Patient Test

Henri Bensussen

Sounds of Saturday—kids yelling, cars honking—weasel into the warm living room through closed blinds. Lydia always keeps the house as dark as possible in summer. In her bones she feels it will remain cool that way even though the thermometer hits 90 before noon. Lydia is sitting on the floor, but not because it is cooler there.

She pulls herself to the phone, brings it down to the floor, and dials the number on her medical insurance card. A woman answers.

"I need some advice," Lydia says, her voice shaking. "My body has fallen asleep."

"Your body?" repeats the woman.

"Everything below the neck," says Lydia.

Another voice comes over the phone, a concerned male voice that wants to know her symptoms. Lydia, embarrassed, one more female complaining of minor pains that mean nothing, begins. "My legs began to fall asleep." She tries to steady herself. "Then it spread up to my waist, and then to my back. I thought I should call before it is too late."

"You're feeling better now?" asks the voice.

"Yes," says Lydia from the floor. The numbness is subsiding, she notes with relief. The question assumes a positive answer and she is happy to comply.

"Call your doctor on Monday," the voice says.

She does as she is told. Her doctor, a woman as perplexed about the episode as Lydia, refers her for a neurological exam. Lydia arrives for her appointment at the hospital a few days later. The neurologist is a young man. Lydia thinks he must be a new doctor, maybe a resident. They're in a windowless box of a room. Every few minutes the air conditioner kicks in and makes a rumbling noise in the ceiling. The doctor looks up nervously when this happens.

"What's the matter?" Lydia asks.

"I work nights at a lab across the street," he says. "Animals escape from their cages and find their way into the ductwork. At night they run back and forth up there—rabbits, rats, mice."

Lydia looks up at the air register in the ceiling. It's dark inside the grating. "Do they ever escape?"

"Not as far as I know." He takes a pen from his pocket.

"What do they eat?"

"Look, we haven't time for chit-chat." He pulls out a form. "I'm going to take your history."

"Can't you read my medical record instead?"

"That?" He glances at the thick folder and back to his form. "No, it's easier this way."

What kind of work does she do, where does she live, with whom? She tells him she lives with a partner. Lydia doesn't mention how her partner responded when Lydia told her what happened: laughed for five minutes, and then had to sit down and drink a Coke. "When your leg falls asleep, it's because of loss of circulation," her partner said. And Lydia had wondered, if those millions of corpuscles weren't streaming through her blood vessels, where were they? Taking a rest break in some hideout? She laughed about it too, afterward.

"Children?" His persistent voice brings her back to their stark room.

"Yes."

"How old?"

She struggles to remember their ages. One married, one not. "Thirty-one, and thirty-six?" She hopes she's remembered correctly, but how would he know? She could make up a whole family, for that matter. She used to want four children, but that was before the first was born and the reality of motherhood set in.

"How old are you?" he asks.

At least she can remember the year of her birth. The U.S. still in the Depression. But he's already moving on to past surgeries. No time for a digression to economic history, her father young and worried about being a good provider.

"Do you take medication?"

"No."

"Vitamins?"

"No. I can never remember to take vitamins." She senses his disappointment. Maybe he is already sure the "episode" she was referred for was due to overdosing on Vitamin A.

"Smoke?"

grandmothers
note

"No."

"Alcohol?" She mentions wine with dinner.

"White wine?"

"Red. I only drink red wine."

"Any, uh, you know, drugs?"

"No." She wonders why red wine means drugs and white wine doesn't.

Body changes come next. "My hands shake more than they used to," she says. "I can't remember things as easily. I have to concentrate—always losing my glasses—and my eyesight is worse; so is my hearing. Sometimes my knee joints hurt." She begins to panic. Maybe he thinks she's in the beginning stages of Alzheimer's. She wants to tell him her friend Marj also forgets things, and she's a year younger.

But now he's asking about sleep patterns. She tells him she often wakes up at night, always around 3:30 a.m. This does not impress him. Nor the intermittent foot and leg cramps that come as she's falling asleep.

He asks about the details of the episode. "Didn't my doctor write it down?" she says.

"I want to hear it in your own words."

Obediently she begins. "First my legs fell asleep. I tried moving them but it didn't help. The same kind of numbness moved up to my waist, my back, my shoulder. I thought I'd better call the clinic. I didn't know if it would stop."

"Could you move?"

"Yes. I just couldn't feel anything."

"Pain?"

"No pain." (What if her brain had become numb? She imagines the prickliness of the awakening brain.)

"Were you hyperventilating?"

She envisions a woman with her face in a paper sack. "No, I was reading."

"Hyperventilating could explain it." His voice expresses disappointment, and Lydia feels how much of a failure she is to him.

He gives her a gown. She is to undress and he will be back with more tests. Except for the noises in the ceiling, the room is quiet, like a motel room: used by everyone, not belonging to anyone.

The doctor returns with a safety pin and a little black bag. He's going to stick her with the open safety pin and she is to tell him if the pinpricks feel the same on each leg, each arm. "Can you feel it on your shoulders, your elbows?" She nods yes each time. He seems intent on pulling the gown off her shoulder as he drags the pin down her arm, while she tries to hold onto this last shred of cloth that covers her naked body.

"Here? Here?" he keeps asking. Finally he stops that and goes into the black bag for a rubber hammer. He hits knees and ankles, watching her reaction time. Her leg jerks up and almost kicks him in the chin. He pulls out a metal prong that he vibrates and then places on various parts of her feet and hands. He uses a hard paddle on the bottoms of her feet.

"I can't find anything that would have caused your problem," he says. "Could've been hyperventilation, could be something with your neck." He gives her a slip for an X-ray "just to make sure" and leaves.

Lydia dresses, relieved to have been freed from her ordeal, and walks to her car. Is this the norm for a post-menopausal divorced woman, two children, one partner? To have indescribable complaints defying logical explanation by doctors young and old, male or female? *We will torture the truth out of you.* She remembers her mother's adage: Don't come to me with your problems. She tosses the X-ray referral into a trashcan.

Early the following morning, with moonlight shining through the bedroom window, Lydia's womb shudders in an orgasmic leap. Suddenly she is in the lab, breathing hard. Her hands shake drunkenly, she gropes for her glasses, knocks over experiments, scatters sheets of data.

"Oh doctor," she mutters through tight lips, "you pinned me under your microscope but couldn't see me, and now I've escaped into the very air you breathe. I haunt you in your glaring room, hide in the dark with the rabbits and rats, race through the air ducts on pattering feet. I'm in a hysterical fever of thought, losing it, losing it…"

Her partner shakes her. "What's with the rabbits? It's the middle of the night."

Lydia feels herself falling out of the ductwork, back into bed, her foot in a cramp. She gets up and reaches for her robe. "One of those dreams. I'm going to make some tea, and try to go back to sleep."

In the kitchen, waiting for the kettle to boil, she picks up a book, puts it down. Her mother nagged her about reading too much. If she had gone out for tennis, or tried to have friends instead of losing herself in a story, would she be a different person? Did her body begin losing its reality because she was caught up in someone else's reality? An out-of-body experience: her partner would have another laugh over that. She pokes her arm, her leg. Nothing is numb except her heart, which continues beating but without sound.

Life Sentence

Judith Day

That damned Linda, she thought, but she really meant that her heart had been broken again by her patient trying to commit suicide again, this time with lots of pills that she had prescribed and a crash of her car into a pole—not a tree, Linda wouldn't hurt a tree—and once again she wouldn't die but this time it will probably take away the real Linda, the Linda who laughs at her jokes at her own expense and who she thought was safe for the weekend, and leave in her place a maimed and mute wheelchair Linda, a vegetable Linda, a flat-faced onion or turnip or potato, at best a sweet potato, as a reminder to her that, a) if only she were able to heal people this wouldn't happen, and b) attempting suicide is not a guaranteed way out, but she nevertheless once again for the hundred thousandth time considered her own possible suicide, her own longing to put to rest forever her own bottomless self-doubt and most of all her own unsleeping nights when she is eating peanut butter and jelly at three-thirty in the morning in an effort to ignore the green faces and slurring sadistic laughter of her own demons that come from her own childhood when her uncle pressed her against a bed and couch and rug and seat of his car and took her to motels where the peeling walls and ceilings, the thin wasted bedspreads, the rank airless air and the locked doors never told the tales of the pressing and licking and shoving and staining and green faces and slurring sadistic laughter that had now followed her for forty years of not killing herself but instead working, working, sincerely and with deep caring in her over-and-over-again broken heart, so that she might heal herself and heal Linda and all the others who came to tell of their uncles, fathers, mothers, grandparents, neighbors, priests, teachers, scout leaders, cousins, therapists, strangers, babysitters, brothers, and sisters, to tell her the story, to speak out loud, even if it was only a whisper or whimper, even if it was a joke or a whistle through a hole in a throat, and be heard.

Creeds

P.J. Schaefer

Doctor Sternham purses his small, pale lips, frowns slightly, hesitates for a moment and then says, "I think you should stop going to church for a while. Put an end to those retreats and the R.E. teaching for now, okay?"

He speaks softly, slowly, sure of his request, but, because he knows his patient's likely reaction, unsure that he should pronounce it so matter-of-factly.

"I can't do that, Doctor." Kathleen O'Reilly stares at the floor, unable to look at Doctor Sternham. She does not like to defy him. *Honor thy father and mother.* She cannot abandon her God, either. *Remember to keep holy the Lord's day.*

Doctor Sternham sees her discomfort, wishes he could avoid causing it, yet knows he must. "Think of it as sick time. You're staying away until you're feeling better."

Thou shalt not bear false witness. "But it's a lie. I'm not so ill that I cannot attend Mass."

Doctor Sternham thinks, "No, only so ill that you almost canceled all Mass appointments for the rest of your life." He waits for Kathi to look at him again and then remarks, "Suppose I talk to Father Nicholas, get permission from him. Then will you stop for a while?"

Kathleen almost smiles, a weak smile, but one that, when studied carefully with the cast of her green eyes, speaks of sarcasm, of a dare. "You can try. If he agrees, then I'll do it. But he won't. He can't." Kathi remembers Father Nicholas, recalls him telling her, "Divorce is wrong. *Thou shalt not commit adultery.* Pray. Pray hard, Kathleen, and the Lord will answer your prayers. Look to the *Bible.* Look there for the answer."

Kathi sees herself looking, reading, reciting: *Turn the other cheek.* She does, so many times that she has no cheek left. Her husband shatters her jaw with a punch and she has to drink and eat through a straw for over a month. *Blessed are the peacemakers.* She keeps the peace, does not strike back, does not speak back, barely speaks at all, hoping not to provoke him.

Doctor Sternham examines Kathi's blank face and distant eyes and knows she has gone away again, to a place he cannot seem to reach, a place he catches only glimpses of. "What are you thinking of now, Kathi?"

"Father, Father Nicholas. He's a good man, a good priest. He guides his flock, the way he's supposed to. He'll be a bishop or a cardinal or the pope someday." Kathleen thinks of the pope. *Go forth and multiply. Do not fornicate.* No birth control, no lust: but Randy wants to. *Wives obey your husbands.* I cannot feed my children. I cannot protect my children. Can you, Father? Will you, Pope John?

She sees young Mike, her oldest of four, lying in a grave, dirt heaped upon him. She sees him running from the long, thick, black pole in his father's hand, not looking where he goes, just going, long tears streaming down his face, his cheeks red, hot with anger and fear, his lips moving, shouting obscenities at his father, and he doesn't see the car. She calls out too late. Mike flies into the air and then lands on the road, his body convulsing until, suddenly, it stops and he lies motionless, dead. Father Nicholas stands over the grave. "*The Lord is my shepherd; I shall not want…*"

"But I do want. I do," Kathi whispers to herself, and Doctor Sternham hears her.

"What is it you want, Kathi?"

Kathi blinks, as if noticing suddenly that Doctor Sternham sits next to her. "I want Michael back. He was too young. I should have saved him."

"How could YOU have saved him, Kathi? Everything is not YOUR fault, not in YOUR control."

Kathi goes away again, watches herself push at Randy, trying to get the pole away from him, and he smashes her back against the wall. The blood springs from her lips. *Thou shalt not kill.* She wants to kill him, but she only stands and shouts, screaming at him to stop. She does not stand between her husband and her son. *He that would follow Me would give up his life for Me.* "But I didn't. I didn't stop him. I didn't get in the way."

"Didn't get in whose way? In between Mike and the car? How could you, Kathi? It was an accident."

"*God's will*? Father Nicholas said that. God's will to take a child only twelve years old? What kind of God has that kind of will?"

Doctor Sternham shifts in his chair, observes the tears spilling over

HOLY BIBLE
Dictionary • Study Helps

the rims of Kathi's eyes, feels, sees her conflict and knows she needs to express it. He believes that conflict brought the blade to her wrists. "Are you angry with God, Kathi?"

I am the Lord, your God; there shall be none before Me. Thou shalt not take the name of the Lord in vain. "No. I am not supposed to get angry with God. He knows all, and we cannot understand His ways. It wasn't God's fault; it was Randy's fault and my fault. I didn't stop him. I should have stopped him."

"Stopped your husband from doing what?" Doctor Sternham eases forward in his chair, pats Kathi's hand gently, trying to keep her with him, trying to coax the scenes of her mind into the open. He can feel the bones of her fingers and hand and looks to her eyes, two, sunken hollows in a gaunt and ravaged face, a vacant, white face, the face of a sixty-year-old instead of the thirty-year- old she is. He sees her irises growing smaller and doesn't want to let Kathi travel away from him again.

"Stopped your husband from doing what?" he repeats, more loudly, so close to her face that his breath upon her moves a strand of hair ever so slightly.

Kathi turns her head, brushes the strand of hair away from her face. *Let him who is without sin cast the first stone. Those who would seek forgiveness must first forgive.* She sits motionless, her eyes closed.

Doctor Sternham stands, paces in front of her several times and then stops in front of her. "Kathi, open your eyes, please. Let's do a little word association; shall we?"

Kathi opens her eyes obediently and waits for his first word. They have played this game before. She thinks it takes no effort, no real thought.

"Happiness."

"Children."

"Marriage."

"Death."

"Death."

"Murder."

"Murder."

"By inaction. Freedom. Release. Retribution. Vengeance." *Vengeance is Mine, sayeth the Lord.* "Mortal Sin." Kathi's voice fades more with each word.

Doctor Sternham crouches in front of Kathi and takes hold of her hands. "Whose mortal sin?"

"Mine. Randy's."

"Randy?"

"Sicko. Creep. Abuser. Murderer." *Thou shalt not kill. Wives, obey your husbands. Thou shalt not commit adultery. Thou shalt not kill.*

"But Randy's dead."

Kathi smiles a satisfied grin. "Yes. God's will, MY will." She sees him choking and herself letting him. She stands and watches. *Thou shalt not kill. An eye for an eye…* She laughs, even, laughs as his face turns red and then blue, laughs as he gasps and coughs and his arms flail about. She laughs still more as he looks at her with panic and fear and pleading in his eyes, the same panic of his son's eyes. *Whatsoever you do to the least of My brothers, that you do unto Me.* A single, silent tear rolls down Kathi's cheek. "*Bless me, Father, for I have sinned.*"

She rubs the pink scar that runs the length of her arm, from wrist to inside side of elbow.

"And I knew what I did."

The Color of Nothing

R. Crawford

A passerby walked hastily along the cobblestone street, shuffling papers and repositioning a messenger bag, tugging at his stiff suit and sporting a disheveled black tie. His shoes hadn't broken in yet and still smelled of leather, reminding him of a collection of literary classics that he had hoped were still in the attic of the house he grew up in. Upon recollecting the great canon with an affectionate, reminiscent smile, a new potency reached him, also from below. His new-smelling shoes had dipped into a shallow trickle of crimson liquid that was so fresh it was still gliding between the crevices of the cobblestone, taxiing little bits of debris along its route. The passerby quickly removed his feet, discovering the host, lying opposite the direction in which the blood trickled.

The rising sunlight glinted the reflective specks on the sidewalk where the cobblestones ended. The passerby's gaze followed a thin and foreboding crack in the concrete—a hairline crack—and at its end lay the delicate and sprawled figure—limbs arranged in right angles, as if measured with precision—unconscious. Her mouth, wide and agape. Little trinkets littered about her: coins that must have burst from her pockets, a cell phone with a broken screen, thin and reaching fissures, white earphones no longer modeling symmetry, as one had shattered. Quite similarly to the earphones, there lay another shattered object nearby, a darker shade of white but not made of plastic, rather, of bone which was the only object not shining in the elongated rays of the sun, due to its lack of luster, opaqueness, and perhaps its loss of dignity. There she lay, undisturbed by the passerby in the fresh suit and crooked tie, who hurried on, relieved to look in any other direction, namely at his now doubly potent shoes.

Biting wind simultaneously swayed and stilled the city; shrieked desperate and pleadingly, we believe, on our behalf. How long it lasted, we think the duration of one night, when, like a child whimpering himself to sleep, the screams regressed to interrupted gasps and lisping susurrations.

We gathered in the hospital, the first time her eyes had opened since the incident—that is the day the world lost its color. Had she been able to smile, she would have done so reassuringly as she told us not to be worried. (She—the object of our gossip and curiosity, the provocation of uncertainty; brooding tension and unease.) Perhaps, she would have said, the world is now *more* colorful. When you observe green, the object is, in all actuality, every color but green. And if we can't see any of the colors, perhaps the world is now all colors. It reflects nothing back. Her eyes were black and shining and themselves absorbed all of the vibrancy that might have otherwise existed. They reflected nothing back.

We don't know why she went mad but there were theories. The enzyme deficiency—low MAOIs can affect one's ability to cope with trauma. (She was never tested for this.) It couldn't help that the Luteal phase of her menstrual cycle coincided with the fullest lunar phase of the moon. Her blood sugar could have been monitored better. Her circulation was poor and resulted in numb fingers and toes when she smoked cigarettes, climaxed during sex, and worse, when she was depressed, because then the numbness crept to her forearms. (So she said.) These minor ailments were trivial and likely unrelated to the madness that ensued. Her family said that they could never satiate her need for attention. She. Their brimming, elusive daughter who had turned the world grey.

He was sitting in the waiting room and had not entered her quarters, where she lay waiting for him. He appeared neither frightened nor especially concerned about the loss of color, and looked as if he rather expected it, like one who has prepared for a coming, violent storm, content now that the winds have just begun to shift—that the sooner it begins the sooner it will pass. It took much prying on our part. We persistently asked him what he knew—of her, of the phenomena.

At first he insisted that we repress our curiosity, that what was broken could not be fixed. The prying might result in a great, gaping tear.

"The world turned bleak, and we know only that it has to do with her."

"What of her?"

"Yes. Tell us: what of her."

He straightened his posture and crossed his legs ankle-to-knee with certain poise. What could he tell us that we didn't already know? Did we lack such awareness that we couldn't see from a distance what he was able to during his brief closeness with her? These are the questions he asked us not with reproach, but matter-of-factly and non-rhetorically. We didn't respond, but gazed with inquiring wide eyes that begged, What of her?

He started over.

"Nearly every time I saw her she was in a state of depression. I would ask, 'Are you often sad?' As often as possible, she'll tell you herself.

"I tried to explain to her that I rarely experience sadness, a pointless emotion. She would say, 'If you don't know sadness, then you haven't read *Poor Folk* properly. And only one who does not know sadness can listen to Shostakovich's Fifth Symphony and not weep.' In fact, my arms, too, were numb when I was sad, I just didn't know how to feel it— how to feel Nothing. 'Numbness isn't feeling,' I'd try to explain, 'that is what makes it numbness.' No, she went on to say that numbness evokes feeling in the very same way that only light can create shadows. But isn't it true that there is no such thing as Nothing? That no complete sentence accurately states, 'Nothing is—' because Nothing is simply not?"

We asked, "Could it be that her sadness, then, was the catalyst for the bleak, fading world?"

"She is severely melancholic, sure, but she embraces all without the slightest bias toward one feeling or another. In fact, when she said she wanted to 'do happy' we agreed that the pills in my bag were enough to induce such a sensation if it could not manifest organically. Ah, a nervous little girl was suddenly before me with shaky hands and confessions of unease and apprehension. I assured her that we would split one, as to dip our feet into happiness rather than plunging into such unfamiliar territory with haste.

"When the warmth filled her (and my, if she isn't always filled, brimming!) she danced all the way to the kitchen for water, singing la-la-las that were bouncing chartreuse and humming along raw siennas. Effervescent whistles, pale pollen yellows. As she walked on her bare tippy toes, ripples of happy (like the crinkling wrinkling lines reaching out from her smiling eyes) appeared under each of her weightless steps. Happiness that ripples concrete floors. Happiness that halts gravity's pull for a hint of a moment."

"If we make her happy again, will our world resume as it was?"

"It isn't happiness or sadness that makes any difference. You can't force

one to feel, because one feels on one's own accord."

Curiosity was ripened, as is often the case, by equal ratios of one part fear, one part fascination. Chins propped on fists; elbows propped on knees. Bodies leaned in as if nearing him would near us to the Truth. Pupils dilated, ready to snatch bright, wise words. Our impatience prompted his lofty scoff; disapproving frown.

"A few hours had passed after we took the pill. The melancholia normally settles in the next day, but perhaps such a small dosage explains why she felt it so soon after. The experience itself was fascinatingly physiological for her in a way that it simply was not for me. As the pill's effect wore off, the warmth was slowly escaping out to her extremities, as if it were a shirt and she were taking it off slowly (and the tingling air exhaled onto her skin), as the retreating fabric exposed, little by little, a shoulder, a bicep, an elbow. Only as it crept past her elbows, she began to panic. She rolled onto her stomach—yes, in my bed, of course—and buried her head into the pillow, writhing and twisting her forearms, alternating which arm would be rubbed, which would do the rubbing. The violent massaging was, I think, meant to salvage the happy she felt in her arms. Her bones cracked, like a tire popping as it runs over a sharp object."

"What did you do?"

"I gently took her arms in my own hands and rubbed the feeling back into them myself. I was sure she would break her own wrists. Small, circular bruises appeared on her the next morning—either from my hands or hers, we couldn't tell."

"You didn't feel the same way?"

"I don't think I have the capacity to feel quite the way she does."

"Capacity?"

"It's my conjecture that the girl recovering just a few doors down the hall, with now black and unfeeling eyes, has exhausted whatever was left to be felt in the world."

Disbelief or denial, whichever describes our reaction best is what ensued, and we searched his darkening face for answers. A momentary pause was followed by, "The fall was no accident. Her request was on my nightstand in handwriting nearly illegible."

"A death letter?" we inquired as one.

"A request."

The Request:

I must not be. I cannot live in photographs, in memory—on this page. Erase me from the Book of Life; no evidence of the pen having touched the paper, no indentations visible from the reverse side. Take back my mother's stretch marks. Wipe away the toe prints that I left on the inside of the windshield (the day we chased the storms to the coast). Place my picture face down.

"She jumped! If you tell us more, we can right it. She is still with us, as you said."

"What is broken, is broken."

"It can always be fixed. Tell us more. What else moved her?"

A corner of the waiting room was now entirely abandoned by the light of several lamps. What were formerly slivers of deep grey, fitted into the crevices, justifying that it was, indeed, the innermost corner where the walls met, were now blackening; growing with great celerity and abysmal subtlety like black mold.

"She would say, 'Each brushstroke sounds of a flirting, quivering a note on the clarinet,' or, 'I loved Heidegger so much that I learned German, despite its odor—German is not a fragrant language.' Those, she loved.

"She focused on art history at the university, which soon developed into a grueling interest in perception—Alberti's window, the vanishing point. She said that she had learned to view the world upside-down—at canted angles and through mirrors, because we cannot rely on our minds—so easily fooled!—and must learn to manipulate the anamorphoses. Ah, but our mere, five senses are grossly limiting only because we allow them to be—that was her supposition. Lazy brains!

"At the gallery where she worked in the summers, she spoke with fervor that ricocheted off of marble floors. Many would gather in to hear about sculptures and frescoes. One of her tours I remember clearly…

"She began her lecture of the painting in terms of the various contrariant colors and the contrast between light and shadow. She went on in greater detail about the lines in the peonies and how they were a different medium—an ink to juxtapose the ethereal wash of the watercolors. 'The line scheme; these arcs along the fold in this petal create movement and a softness that—like here, do you see the composition she chose? The abrupt curvature in the table manipulates the way you understand the piece. The influence of lines creates movement and perceived velocity.'

"As she spoke, the dimples outside of her lips contoured parenthetically and little crow's feet defected outward from almond eyes."

"But they weren't drawn in India ink like the peonies," he explained. "Rather, the wrinkles were ironed and replaced with her familiar, pensive frown, and the impression of the ego line, forever scored on her forehead. Strands fell from the loosely tied back hair and again modified her composition; softening the harsh, descending line of her jaw and broadening an unfamiliar disposition. I wondered if her beloved da Vinci could explain how she appeared farthest away when she was still within my physical reach. If this gradual retrograde was not a grand illusion created by lines or the vanishing point, perhaps it was Isaac Newton who I could refer to on the laws of physics—the constant motion, absconding."

The painting evoked feeling (of course!) we suggested. He denied us any reassurance on the matter. Is art not fulfilling? To be like her—filled and brimming, as he said, that was the remedy! He looked past us. His blank stare revealed his reluctance to provide false hope. We were left to fend for ourselves.

The music was sprightly azure and alternately contrasted by the slightest hints of sombre sepia. We visualized the rising intonation, climbing ever vermillion and descending to what—can't you see? The color that we knew, we could describe it but somehow could not see properly in the mind's eye—like describing a former childhood friend, who certainly did have tan skin and blond hair, freckles on her nose and cheeks, one even on her lip, and yet you still cannot *see* her when you close your eyes. Now that luminosity could be heard and felt and even tasted, licked with the part of the tongue sensitive to sweetness. It surged into our consciousness, simultaneously warming and cooling both internally and externally, all and everything.

Didn't we float on our backs despite the burning of the sapphire and splash each other playfully? We gargled fuchsia, like children playing with mouthwash in the bathroom, and hydrated ourselves with citrine. We drank the bright shades greedily and they ran down our chins— faces stained with running make-up of *Everycolor*! If we believed that it would persist, perhaps it would (isn't that what the law of attraction leads us to believe?).

That was our one hope—hope as the equivalent of a mirage in the wasteland.

Our hope that, when she ceased perhaps the color would fully return. Rather, after the color faded, the darkness stormed in, and eventually, Nothing.

Red is for Later

Farah Ahamed

Those who frequent Kisementi are familiar to me. I know the street vendors who wear necklaces of mobile phones around their necks and roam the car park. I recognise the expatriates in their Pajeros and Troopers, NGO slogans pasted on their cars: "End Poverty, Together." They come to Kisementi to stand on the pavement outside Fat Boyz for a *one one*, a Nile or Bell lager. This is their regular *chimeza*, to discuss Ugandan politics and sport. Then there are the shoppers; mothers, in Toyotas and Hondas with children in the back seat, who go to the Payless supermarket, two or three times a week, rushing in and out. Most times I listen to the radio as I watch the chaotic congestion of *boda bodas*, *special hires*, *taxis*, *matatus* and private cars. I do this every day, for a few minutes or sometimes even for a few hours. I watch them park, shop, go to the bar and then drive away. Nobody asks me, I never explain. Piers never comes here and I don't tell him I do. Last week I asked him if we could paint the living room wall red. He replied, "Red is for later!" and ruffled my hair. I pushed his hand away.

In the middle of the parking lot there is a kiosk made from galvanised iron sheets; a girl in a blue and white school uniform is buying roasted maize wrapped in newspaper. She takes a bite, it burns her mouth, she spits it out and covers her mouth with her hand. Red is for later.

Kisementi is a shopping centre, in Kololo, a suburb in Kampala which is, by default rather than design, a "U" shape. The top floors of the buildings are residential, the ground floors have shops. On the left are the Banana Boat, a store for locally made handicrafts and the Crocodile restaurant. In the middle of the "U" are the Fat Boyz pub and the Payless supermarket and on the right is a Christian Bookshop.

Yesterday, we were at a dinner party with Nicole and Marc and when I looked around, I recognised many faces from Kisementi. I knew how often they shopped, how long they took, how many bags of groceries they carried and who went to Fat Boyz. I was introduced to some of them, but nobody said "I've seen you somewhere, haven't I? Your face is familiar!" I was gratified; I was invisible, even after sitting in the car park and seeing them every day, they hadn't seen me. Nicole interrupted my thoughts. Her pale pink silk dress gave her an angelic look, and in my black chiffon, I felt like a witch, harbouring the secrets of shoppers.

"So darling, what's new?" she said, patting her bob.

"Not much, we're re-decorating and I plan to paint the living room wall red."

She turned to Piers, "Do you like it?"

"Red is for later," Piers replied, not looking at her or me.

Nicole arched her eyebrow at me, I didn't respond; she wasn't the only one who didn't understand.

Piers put his hand on Marc's elbow and led him away to the bar.

"Let's get a drink; we're going to Thailand…!"

"You're going to Thailand?" Nicole twisted her lips.

The lights running through the tree above our table changed colour every few minutes and the background music from the guitarist wafted across the garden. That was the first time I'd heard Piers mention Thailand. I watched the woman at the next table stirring her cocktail. She was the one who always parked badly at Kisementi. Nicole tapped my arm, I pulled my thoughts back to her.

Later that night, after the party, as we drove home, we passed Kisementi. I fidgeted in my seat and turned my head to look at the car park. There were no cars parked under the street lights and the Fat Boyz green and orange neon sign "Warm beer and soggy burgers" was off.

"What are you looking at?" Piers asked.

"What about the wall?"

"We're going to Thailand!"

"What about the wall?"

"Red is for later!" he joked.

I kept quiet, I would go to Kisementi tomorrow.

I called Nicole the next morning. "It's about Piers, I need to tell you something…

"Is this about Thailand? Has he changed his mind?"

"No, it's about him. He doesn't listen to what I say anymore!"

"Don't be silly, how can that be possible?"

"It's true, didn't you notice yesterday?"

"What do you mean?"

"You heard him say 'Red is for later' didn't you?"

"He was joking…"

"But it never used to be like that. I don't know what's happened…"

"All marriages go through this after a few years, it's the ordinary. You're worrying too much. You'll find your own way to deal with it. All men are like that, ask anybody!"

I didn't believe her. After a few minutes I hung up, when I heard Pier's footsteps outside the study.

The next evening when Piers came home, I was in the garden; it was about seven o'clock, and the sun had just started setting. I waved as he entered the house; he waved back. I carried on weeding and digging, it had been a hot day and the air was still humid. The soil was damp and the warm, heady scent of the night blooming Jasmine filled the air. No wonder it is called Queen of the Night. I lay down on the freshly cut grass and looked at the sky. It changed from light blue to deep blue with streaks of pink and yellow and then very quickly it became dark. I saw something flying around a tree, maybe it was a lost bird looking for its nest, but then it was a bat. The street lights came on and moths, flies, locusts, *nsenene*, and other night insects buzzed around the low garden lamps. Crickets whistled, somewhere in the grass, a few feet away. The clouds moved slowly and the moon came out from behind them. I went inside and stood by the study door, Piers hadn't heard me; he was engrossed in watching the news.

"I uprooted most of the garden and replanted the pots. I weeded all the rose beds!" I flapped a small fern which I brought in to show him. Its roots were white, thin and straggly, like an old woman's hair.

He turned his head in my direction, taking in my muddy shoes and trousers rolled up at the ankles. "Oh good, are we ready for dinner now?"

I looked at my hands; they were covered in soil and my fingernails had a line of brown mud. The back of my shirt was damp. I pushed my hair back and felt bits of grass. Piers was already absorbed by the television again. I waited a few seconds and then threw the plant at him. He ducked and it landed on the floor.

"Is there a problem?" he turned to look at me, his eyebrows raised.

"Damn you Piers! It's almost ten o'clock and all you can say is…what

about dinner?"

He switched off the television and crossed his arms. "Why is dinner so late?"

"Dinner? What about the fact I've been in the garden all evening?"

"Well, what about it?"

"Why don't you listen to what I say?"

"I always listen! What do you mean?" he shook his head, his eyebrows knotted.

"No, you don't. When I ask you a question you don't respond or you give me an unrelated answer."

"I always do, you're the one who never listens and does strange things!"

"What does that mean?"

"Oh, I don't know…" he uncrossed his arms and stretched, "Like, lie on the grass and stare at the sky? And…"

"What?"

"You disappear for hours…"

"When?" My stomach tightened. Had he been spying on me?

He stood up, pulled a leaf from my hair, opened my palm and put it there. "Like tonight, you disappeared in the garden, nobody gardens at this hour!"

I shrugged.

"Look, it doesn't matter, I don't want to argue. Let's eat dinner, we'll talk tomorrow."

He sat down again and switched on the television. I was relieved. At least he didn't know about Kisementi.

At breakfast Piers said nothing about our argument. I saw that my nails were still brown.

"Pass me the sugar please." He put down his newspaper and handed me the butter dish. I took a teaspoon of butter and stirred it in my tea. Oil globules floated to the surface. I looked up, Piers was watching me. He pushed back his chair and eyed the oily mixture in my cup.

"I'll ring you. Bye."

"I'll order the paint?"

"Later!" he said, one foot out the door.

I worked at my desk all day and forgot about Piers. I finished some emails and made a few phone calls and by the afternoon I was tired. Our study was on the first floor and from it I had an unobstructed view of the garden. I picked up the plant, which still lay on the rug and wondered if I should go back to the garden for a few hours and re-plant it, but the sun was setting and it would soon be dark.

From the window I saw the *Kaloli, Marabou* storks come to rest on the trees. They gently descended with their black cloak-like wings wide open which closed around their long, skinny, white legs when they landed on the tree tops before they swooped down to the grass where I had lain yesterday. Their pointed beaks protruded from their bald white heads and their pink throat sacs hung loosely like amulets around their hairy, scrawny necks which retracted and stretched, as they moved noiselessly in the grass scavenging on dead insects. There were dozens of them and at dusk they looked like pre-historic vultures. I couldn't bear to watch them.

The study has a bookshelf and a writing bureau on which there was a haphazard pile of books. I rearranged them and noticed as if for the first time, the different textures of paper in the books; glossy, dull, matt, smooth, wrinkled, rough. Some had embossed bumpy pictures and script, others were slick and shiny. Some felt warm and others cold. I touched and held them to my cheek. Each book smelt different, a specific grassy mustiness, even slightly acidic and one even had a hint of vanilla. I ran my fingers on the window sill and felt a soft powdery film on my fingertips. The dust always collected in Kampala.

I lay down on the rug and stretched, feeling the lush weave, the soft wool texture against my body. I closed my eyes. What had happened between us? Why didn't he listen anymore? The room was silent, there were no sounds coming from outside. I went out onto the balcony, the cold, uneven, gritty grain of the hard stone tiles on the soles of my feet reassured me. The muted preying birds had gone. I watched the sky as the clouds became grey and heavy, it would rain soon; I could smell it. It was nine o'clock when the phone rang. It was Piers; he'd be home very late, I shouldn't wait for him. He hung up before I could respond. I was free.

I parked my car opposite Fat Boyz and turned on the radio; Capital FM was playing jazz and blues. The car park was congested; it was the start of the weekend. The Christian bookshop had been converted into a bar and a barbecue joint; the revellers crowded around white plastic tables and chairs on the pavement and feasted on locally brewed beer and *mchomo*. On my left, a man in a checked shirt leaned against his car and lit a cigarette; a late night street vendor approached him and they haggled over the price of a bunch of *matooke*.

"You're my last customer, *ssebo*, then I go home. Promote me!" he coaxed.

A car drove up and parked on my right. Under the street lights, I could see the woman talking on her mobile phone while she flicked her hair in the rear view mirror. I felt at ease in the familiarity and the anonymity. A car honked and pulled up in front of me; it was the woman who always parked badly, the one from the party. I rolled down my window.

"Are you planning on leaving anytime soon?" she asked. I was about to answer but the neon Fat Boyz sign flashed orange to green, and I was distracted.

"Leaving whom? To go where?" I asked confused, but she wasn't talking to me; she was talking to the woman on the mobile phone.

"No, I am not, but you should look where you are going!" the woman on the phone said to her, flicking her hair.

I rolled up my window before they could speak to me and switched off the radio. The woman on the mobile phone went to the Crocodile Restaurant and the other, after parking her car, half on the pavement and half in a pothole, went to the Payless supermarket.

A few hours later I awoke to the sounds of loud music. The crowd on the pavement outside Fat Boyz was a happy one. It was Friday evening. The revellers stood around the *chimeza's* with their brown lager bottles. Payless had closed and the Crocodile restaurant was dark, but the car park was full. I thought I saw Piers standing outside Fat Boyz, but it couldn't be, he never came here. I pushed my seat back.

Then it began to rain. First it drizzled and then it poured. Everyone rushed to take cover inside Fat Boyz; the *chimezas* were overturned as the party was interrupted. The car windows steamed up. I put the wipers on. I shivered and my stomach rumbled. The wipers swished back and forth, the rain did not look like it would stop. It was after twelve, Piers hadn't called.

I drove home and called Piers, he said he'd be home as soon as he could. I called Nicole, she didn't answer. I stood at the window watching the rain. Small brown locusts, nsenenes, hopped about on the balcony and around the garden lamps. The night watchman, in his raincoat and a plastic bag on his head had a small fishing net with which he was trying to trap them. The street lights flickered in the distance. I ate some crackers and cheese and lay on the rug; its soft pile and the dark room comforted me. I dozed off. I awoke with a jolt when a car honked and a faraway voice shouted, "Are you leaving?" I sat up and hugged my knees; the room was quiet, the rain had stopped.

I looked out of the window. The corpses of rain insects lay strewn on the wet window ledge and floating in the small pools of water on the balcony floor. The night watchman was seated near the garden lamp, de-winging and breaking the legs off the *nsenenes*. I called Piers, he did not answer. As I drove out the gate, the *askari* tapped on the car window.

"Madam, you want *nsenenes*?" He smiled and offered me his gift. "They're ready to be fried and can be tasty. You try…"

He unrolled the damp newspaper and showed me the clump of brown, dead locusts, without wings or legs. I felt a lump in my throat, I shook my head.

Kisementi was empty; the parking lot was filled with puddles. I parked opposite the Fat Boyz, under the dim street lamps. The lights inside the pub were low and the music was getting fainter; there were a few people on the pavement. I checked my doors; they were all locked. The windows were all up, I was safe. I found some chocolate in the glove box. I ate it and leaned back in the seat. There were dead insects on the windscreen, their wings stuck in the wipers. It was past four in the morning. I would wait for Piers to call; I turned on the radio and shut my eyes. When the phone rang, it was almost five o'clock.

"Where are you?" His voice was angry.

"Hi, Piers."

"Why aren't you home?"

"I'm at Kisementi!"

"I even checked the garden, the *askari* told me you'd gone out."

"Ask me why I come here every day"

"Where?"

"Come get me!"

He kept quiet, the neon lights flash orange and green, and after a few seconds he hung up. An hour went by and the lights inside the pub went off. Then the neon sign stopped flashing. Fat Boyz were going home.

Piers didn't call so I drove back to the house. The garden was quiet but for the *askari* packing his things to go off duty. The house was in darkness, except for one light in the study. I turned the key in the front door and as I did, the study light went off.

I waited, there was no sound. I could creep into bed next to Piers, he wouldn't say anything in the morning and if I did, he wouldn't hear me. I could sleep in the car; but where? Kisementi? I left the key in the front door and went back to the car.

At the Sheraton I asked for a room, checked in and took a shower. I boiled some water in the travel kettle and made some tea. The powder milk formed clumps when I shook it into the hot water and didn't disintegrate when I stirred. There were stray wings of the rain insects near the bed side lamp. I cried until I could smell the mustiness in the pillow.

Piers called me the next day, annoyed. "Where are you?"

I didn't respond.

"Hello?"

"You don't listen to me anymore!" "What are you talking about?"

"The red wall, you don't give me a proper answer!"

"We're going to Thailand, you need a change of scene…"

"Why do I need a change of scene?"

He hung up, as if he hadn't heard me. I lay on the bed and wondered what to do next.

I stayed in the hotel for a week. I bought a few clothes, went to work and drove to Kisementi. Piers didn't call me again, so I rented a furnished flat. I sent him a text saying I needed my books. The taxi man told me Piers had left them in a cardboard box in the garden and he had to rescue them one at a time as it had rained the night before and the base of the box had given way. I drifted from one day to the next. I unpacked the box and arranged the books on a shelf even though the pages were stuck together and the covers were crumpled, damp and browned with mud. A bookmark fell from the pages of one of the books; an old birthday card from Piers.

A week later Nicole phoned, I told her what had happened.

"It's the most natural thing for a marriage to change. It can't always be romance like at first blush. Maybe he's bored of the novelty of a wife?" she paused, and took a breath, "Maybe you're bored too?"

"Of course I'm not bored of Piers!"

"Maybe you are, maybe you're not. But you should go to Thailand, you'll feel better after a holiday…"

"Forget about Thailand! Why doesn't he listen to me like he used to?" I tried to explain again, but she hung up.

After work, the following day, I drove to Kisementi. I listened to Capital FM's sun downer count down and the traffic updates and watched the familiar scene. I recognised the man who usually drove a Pajero, in a different car. Today he had a Toyota salon. He parked and went to the alley between the Crocodile and Banana Boat where there are two stalls; one selling pirated DVDs and the other a unisex hair dressing salon. The owners were sitting in the corridor on wooden stools reading the newspaper.

"Haircut and DVD, Sir?" one of them shouted. He nodded and was ushered into the DVD shop; he shook his head; he wanted a shave first.

The kiosk had a queue of school children waiting for roasted maize. Somebody honked, I didn't respond. I thought I saw a man who looked like Piers, but it couldn't be; he never came to Kisementi. Then the man was walking towards my car. He knocked on the window, I rolled it down, confused.

"What are you doing here?" I gripped the steering wheel.

He looked the same; it had only been three weeks.

"Come home!"

I kept quiet.

"Our tickets are booked for Thailand."

"Thailand?"

He nodded, the neon sign flashed behind him, first orange, then green, then orange again, then green. A street vendor with flowers sidled up.

"*Ki kati, ssebo, …*flowers ?"

"I'll buy all, how much?"

"*Weebale, weebale…!*" the man smiled.

Piers put his hand in through my window and lifted the lock for the back door. He opened it and put the flowers on the back seat. "So, will you come home?" his voice was softer.

"I come here every day, for hours."

"I'll be waiting..."

I watched as he reversed out of the parking spot and then as he drove past my car, he honked and waved.

I stayed in the car park and watched the shoppers and revellers. The sweet, heady scent of lilies filled the car. I ate some roasted peanuts, they made me thirsty. The hours went by, the pub lights went out and the neon sign "Warm beer and soggy burgers" faded. Piers didn't call or come back. It was after midnight, the street lights flickered dimly. It didn't look like it would rain tonight.

My Name is Not Not Jane

Nikki Vogel

Like a man limping, but at different paces. Fast. Slow. Medium. Ca-clump. Ca-clump.

"Can't you hear it?"

Doctor Steve's thin lips press together.

"It's hard for me to know when he's close because I can only hear his footfalls some of the time."

Doctor Steve, incidentally, is mad. His name is Dr. Fatuous, he told me, or was it Faustus? But immediately afterwards he told me that he wanted us to be friends, to have a relaxed and conversational relationship, and so I should call him Steve. So far I have declined this informality. It is imperative to be careful with mad people.

"We've discussed this before, Jane."

He gets up from behind the desk, closes the blinds. He knows I worry about who might be out there. I spend too much time looking for the limping man. Doctor Steve wants my full attention. I think he's falling in love with me.

"What you hear is the sound of your own heart beating. It is a symptom of anxiety. Try using the relaxation techniques I've shown you."

One of the slats in the blinds is stuck to another. It makes a small opening. I stare at it. He sighs, gets up and adjusts the slats so that the blinds form a clean blank surface.

"Jane, would you like to sit or lie down today?"

Because he's mad he keeps calling me Jane even though I have told him many times that it is not my name. "Jane is a very plain name." I sit down.

"Why do you say that?" He takes off his glasses and rubs his eyes.

"Janes live plain lives. The laws of rhyme say so. Although one often sees a Jane run. Is running plain do you suppose? Janes have fun with Dick." I blush and close my eyes. When my eyes are closed he can't see me, or I can't see him seeing me. Either way, I keep my eyes closed until my cheeks cool down.

There is a barren plain, the kind of plain by which the word barren is defined—it is both incapable of producing offspring and mentally dull. Though. Just though, clouds boil overhead and, perhaps, far into the distance, does the land rise ever so slightly? Hills? Mountains? A horse rears at the head of a procession, advancing across the barrenness of the barren plain, prancing on spindle legs. Its companions march behind, led ever onward over empty beige sand.

"Where did you go just now?"

"Elephants. I went to elephants. Impossibly tall ones on spindle multi-jointed legs."

He turns his head to look at what I'm seeing. It is a painting. No, not a painting. A reproduction of a painting. A facsimile. Which itself was a reproduction or representation of a place where the painter had been. Where Dali had been. I hope never to travel to that land, even in a dream. That Doctor Steve has this surrealist picture on his wall speaks about the state of his mind. Here, of all places, where the droolers live. I am serious; there are droolers.

The elephants are beasts of burden and carry cargo—an obelisk, a woman, marble, clutching her own naked bosom, a palace with the nude torso of a giantess in the window.

"Windows are the eyes to the soul of a building." Clearly this building has a mote in its eye. A large, busty woman in its eye.

He doesn't comment one way or the other.

"Jane, how have you been feeling since the last time we met?" His eyes are like the soul of a building. I'm worried that he is in love with me. He cares so much about my feelings, only ever wants to talk about me. I don't even bother to remind him that my name is not Jane.

I don't like this side of the desk. On his side, the power side, the chair fits neatly under the surface. I frown. He stares. We remain silent. Who will break first?

There are these lovely buildings. Uniform. Three windows and then two. Three, then two. Repetition in neutral tones. Burgundy shingles on the rooftops. They spread across the horizon line and scoot towards me, perspectively. Perceptively? They would be very pleasant, very pleasant indeed, if it were not for the men. There are men in bowlers and trench coats everywhere. Falling from the sky. No, that's not quite right. They hover. By the windows. In the windows.

"Have you noticed, Jane, how you avoid answering my questions?"

I frown. I stare. He cleans his glasses again.

"Imagine if you opened your drapes one day and men were hovering there." I mimic the action of opening drapes and then throwing my hands up in alarm. "I don't like these reproduced men living in their reproduction of an original. Where did Magritte travel to that he saw such a thing? It's like this place. There is always someone hovering. Lurking, not lingering. Lingering implies a sort of faithful waiting. Hopefulness. The people here, they're lurkers. You can't trust a man in a trench coat." I slap my hand down on his desk. He jumps slightly.

"If the paintings are too distracting I can take them down for your appointments. I thought you'd enjoy the art. You were a curator."

Curator. From the Latin cūrā. To care for, attend to. Caring is as dangerous as men in trench coats.

"Is it the levity of drunkenness that allows them to hover?"

"Do you think today is a good day to talk about drunkenness, Jane?" He pounces.

There are certain topics that he's most interested in.

And Jane again. Clearly he's not in his right mind. Right. Mind. Off to the left somewhere. That's where his mind has gone. And he's left-handed. He makes notes on a pad of lined paper, writing with his left hand. Twins are often left-handed. I read that somewhere. I wonder if his twin is unbalanced as well. I wonder if his twin is smallish and blond and wears glasses. Maybe not identical. No reason to think he isn't a paternal twin. He's quite paternal toward me.

"What do I know about drunkenness? I don't drink."

"Is there a reason you don't drink? Try not to avoid the topic. Just say what comes to mind."

"I want to answer your questions, I really do." This is a lie. "I can't help it. There is a void. In my mind. There, where the answers to your questions are." I stand up. Move toward the window and then away. Toward and then away. "Do you hear him? He's coming. He's limping."

I don't want to call him Steve. If he's not in love with me then I want to address him more formally. Damn it. I wish I had paid closer attention to his name, but that's how it is in the beginning. I never know who's going to be important and who isn't. When to pay attention to a name, and when it's not worth the mental effort. When to say enough is enough. It's embarrassing after all this time to have to ask him. It might hurt his feelings and he's always so worried about mine.

"It's okay, Jane. Sit down. Relax. Try a few deep breaths. That's right. Good." He smiles to show his approval. "Let's change the subject. Are you still experiencing side effects from your medication?"

His coffee smells good. I long for a cup of my own, and though he might be in love with me, or not, he doesn't offer. Not because he's unkind, or thoughtless. Who is more thoughtful than Doctor Steve? Am I comfortable? Would I prefer to lie down or sit? Eyes open or closed? How am I feeling? Solicitous, he is. But—

But, there was an incident. When we first met. He spoke to me in an inappropriate manner. He pushed. I warned him that I would have to report him. He kept pushing. Asking me questions about—

"None of your business." The first time I said it forcefully, thinking that this would be enough to redirect his interest. I mean one has certain expectations with regards to social norms. It's disconcerting, troubling even, when people act outside the norms. That is why norms exist. To act within. Maybe he has ADD, or ADHD, and doesn't interpret the visual and verbal cues properly. This only just occurred to me. What if he has a behavioral disorder in addition to being mentally unstable? He could be a dangerous man, especially in love. This happens sometimes. People in love become dangerous. People we love become dangerous.

"None of your business." The second time I shouted it. He just kept pushing. Asking me—

"None of your fucking business." They say three time's the charm, and when I shouted my response the third time I mentally punctuated the sentence with multiple exclamation marks and threw my coffee cup at him. It didn't hit him. He has good reflexes, our Doctor Steve, and moved his head out of the path of the cup in a timely fashion. The liquid, not particularly hot because I like a lot of cream, splattered the front of his shirt however and ever since I have been prohibited from drinking coffee in his presence. If he loved me wouldn't he at least offer me a cup of coffee? In a paper cup if he's worried about sharp shards of ceramic? Do I even want him to love me? This, it seems to me, is the important question.

The fact that he called me Jane again makes me feel better about forgetting his surname. It occurs to me to ask one of the hoverers that are forever about. One of them must know.

"I am very thirsty all the time. I hope it is not a symptom of some terrible disease." I know that I'm perfectly healthy. I just like to think of him thinking that I think I'm sick.

"That is nothing to worry about, a simple side effect. Perhaps we should get you a refillable water bottle so you can sip throughout the day."

See that, how he refers to himself in the plural. What did I tell you?

In front of the rearing horse and the spindle-legged elephants, a naked man cowers holding up a cross. The horse's shoes are on backwards, or its hooves are on backwards and the shoes are on correctly. It is difficult to tell. It is difficult to know what is in the mind of another. No matter how well you know them. No matter how many years you have known them. No matter how many years you were married to them. Their eyes are only windows into buildings. Nothing more.

Dr. Friday is talking again. Faustus? Fuck sakes, Steve. Doctor Steve is talking again. Pressing himself into my mind. "We have to talk about what happened, Jane, if you're ever going to get better."

If I had a cup of coffee I'd throw it again. Get better? There is no better. There are only empty houses.

"Did you know that this one is a self-portrait?" I gesture to the third reproduction Doctor Steve had placed on the wall. It's called *The Son of Man*.

"I didn't know that."

"Magritte investigated the visible through his art. The visible that is concealed and the visible that is seen."

He wears a bowler. And a trench coat. Stands in front of a brick wall, waist high. The ocean is calm behind him, but clouds hang heavy in the sky. His is wearing a red tie. A striking red tie.

"That tie makes a slash of color. So red. Like blood. No. Maybe not blood. Blood goes everywhere. Blood was everywhere."

"What comes to mind when you think about blood?" Doctor Steve leans forward just slightly, then sits back again. Makes some more notes.

"What is it about this man and the trench coats?" I shout. I sweep my hand toward the painting of the hovering men, brushing them away. "My husband had a trench coat. Men in trench coats are not to be trusted."

"Would you like to talk about this? It seems important to you. Why aren't men in trench coats to be trusted?"

"There is a painting by Salvador Dali. It hangs in St. Petersburg. Not Russia. Florida. It has a cumbersome title: 'Gala Contemplating the Mediterranean which becomes a Portrait of Abraham Lincoln.' You have to relax, trick your eyes, allow them to see the way a portrait of Lincoln is disguised as a window overlooking the sea. Or vice versa."

"I'm familiar with that one. What makes you bring it up? Would you like to talk about how the paintings are connected for you?"

"Salvador loved Gala so very much. He would never have done anything to harm her, or their children. Did they have children?"

"I don't know."

"Well, he wouldn't have harmed them. He loved her too much."

Doctor Steve makes more notes.

I wonder if that trick of the eye can be applied elsewhere. Wouldn't that be a useful skill, to trick the eye into seeing what's hidden? I try it on Doctor Steve. Try to see what he's hiding.

"Doctor. Steve, can you hold perfectly still?"

He pushes back from his desk with both hands as though he will rise. He stays there for a moment, and then scoots back to his original position.

He says something but I can't hear him properly. The limping man is very close. My God, he must be right behind me! I jump up. He's not there. I pretend that I got up to take a closer look at *The Son of Man*. Why paint a man with an apple in front of his face?

The limping man is close. Is he hiding behind the apple?

"This apple brought no knowledge." I look at Doctor Steve with what I hope is a sincere expression. I want him to believe me. "There is no knowing. He can't see around it." One can never know, really know, what grows at the heart of another. It might split and release a butterfly. Or a spindle legged horse with backwards feet. "There is no knowing if the trench coat hides the kind of man that—"

"Jane. You're crying. Can you verbalize why you're sad?"

"Doctor!" I still can't find it in my mind, his surname. He doesn't love me and I will not call him Steve. I bolt away from *The Son of Man*, move toward the window. The limping man is back. Ca-clump. He's moving quickly now. Ca-clump. He's close. I know he will be wearing a trench coat.

"I went to London once." He has a box of tissues on his desk. I use one and then another. I don't see a garbage can so I put them in the pocket of my sweater. My hands are shaking. I sit back down. I want to sit on his side of the desk. This side feels wrong, awkward, but I know from experience that he will not allow this.

"You went to London once."

"There were many, many art galleries." And men. In trench coats. "I held the hand of someone small. Child sized. It felt very good, very fine, to have that small hand in my own."

I close my eyes. My hand holds an invisible one.

"This is good, Jane. Can you keep going?"

I stand and turn my back to him. Give him the silent treatment. A bloodless wound for his constant pressing. I can hear him breathing. How desperately he loves me. How desperately he wants me to tell him—

"One painting I *remember* well." I make the word an admonishment. "Perhaps you could get a copy, a descendant of it, to hang on your wall. Add to your collection."

"Can you describe this painting to me?"

I put my finger between the slats of the blinds, tempt fate, think about a peek, but yank it back. What if the limping man is on the other side? What if he has sharp teeth?

Sharp repressed teeth. Ca-clump. Ca-clump.

"A Greek woman, from ancient times, stands in a doorway holding a drapery to one side." I mimic her gesture and sweep aside an invisible curtain.

"Behind her there are shadows, tinged with red. Even the structure is rust colored. And in the shadows, the faintest hint of a sinister face. Her gown is meticulously rendered, chiaroscuro bringing each fold into high relief."

My arm, still holding aside the invisible curtain, drops. I clasp a small invisible hand in my own larger one.

"Light from an unseen source makes red highlights on the folds of her gown, but only from the waist down. Only where her womb is. Her cheeks, too, are red, but with hectic vitality. She rests her other hand on the long, long handle of a two-headed axe."

I raise my free hand above waist height, but lower than shoulder, showing him how long the axe handle is. I rest my hand there on top of memory. In my other hand, still, the small remembered one.

Doctor Steve, for his part, is silent. Waiting. He lets me lead the dance. I'm glad he doesn't love me.

"The truest red, the reddest of reds, pools beneath the axe head, dripping down the sides of its blades. It is Clytemnestra. She has murdered Agamemnon for sacrificing their daughter Iphigenia."

"What was the name of the painting?"

"Sophie asked the same question. I didn't want to tell her it was called 'After the Murder.'"

"Who was Sophie?"

"Her daughter."

"Your daughter?"

"No, her daughter."

"Jane, can you tell me the name of your daughter?"

"I never had a daughter. My name is not Jane."

Catbot's in the Cradle

Vivian Papp

Martha sat in her workshop on the torn-up, once-beautiful chaise lounge that had formerly held the bottoms of two generations before her. Like Aunt Sadie, a spinster who never failed to remember Martha's birthdays with left over makeup samples from her days as an Avon lady.

Martha had, at one point, amassed a collection of nearly three hundred minuscule lipsticks in shades ranging from Icy Pink to Deep Merlot. She had tried to use them from time to time, but the colors often were so out of fashion that they only attracted jeers and snide remarks from her classmates.

Martha remembered once when she was heading over to confirmation practice wondering if Jeff would be there, and suddenly realized she had no makeup on! She fished around in her bag only to find a single micro-lippie in Crimson Red. She quickly smudged a bit onto her eyelids and lips, hoping that Jeff would find her irresistible. As she hurried into the basement of Mt St Mary's Church, she blushed profusely realizing she was late and everyone was already seated, munching hungrily on the leftover donuts provided for them by the parish nuns. She sat down next to her friend, Kathy, who looked at her quizzically.

"Is that red eye makeup? Wow, interesting."

Martha had just nodded, thinking how funny it would be if everyone started wearing red eye makeup. She has wondered if she should mention this idea to Aunt Sadie. Maybe she would take her under her wing and teach her the trade. Martha had always been fascinated by makeup and beauty, even though she was as plain as plain could be. When she came home, she called Aunt Sadie to tell her about her idea, but Aunt Sadie just laughed and said something about skin tone and shading that went right over Martha's head. She did understand that her idea was not as trend-setting as she thought, and this realization was further qualified by the comments and odd looks she received Monday morning in school.

"Red is really your color." Martha always had difficulty picking up on social cues which was unfortunate for her since she seemed to be the topic of gossip that morning. Everyone was staring and whispering. Except for Jeff. Even with this newfound infamy, she remained invisible to him.

She did not, however, escape the notice of Marco, the nerd who seemed to think they were good friends, and had recently been hinting at something more. This idea made Martha nauseous. The next weekend, Aunt Sadie decided to give Martha a makeover, even though her mom (Sadie's older sister) did not approve of makeup or anything that remotely smacked of narcissism. After the expert application of cosmetics and a bit of time spent under the hot bonnet, Martha was revealed to be something of a beauty. At least that's what Aunt Sadie led her to believe. Her mother walked in and deflated any confidence that had dared to appear.

"You look like a clown. A slutty whore clown. Take that shit off of your face and get the dishes done." She didn't seem angry, just disappointed. Martha never wore makeup or thought of herself as pretty ever again. Aunt Sadie came around less and less after that.

Martha's mom, Gloria, had been a pageant girl and a majorette when she was younger. Most of her beauty had faded long ago, but sometimes, when she was just the right amount of drunk so her face softened without distorting, a glimmer of it could still be seen. She wished for nothing more than to have been born less attractive. It had caused her nothing but heartache. Martha was her third child from one of her four failed marriages, she was not sure which one, since a few of them overlapped each other. She was reasonably sure who her father was though. Not that it mattered, since she hadn't seen him since Kindergarten. Her mom made sure that the passion with which her men loved her was ultimately equaled by the passion with which they grew to despise her. She often told Martha how lucky she was to not have been burdened with beauty. Martha didn't really see it that way, of course. After her mother died, she had gone to live with Aunt Sadie. She brought the chaise along with her. A few years after that, her Aunt Sadie died, leaving Martha everything she owned including the chaise which now supported the 58 year old widow and mother to a dead child.

In college, Martha realized she was gifted in science and math and was particularly fond of the field of robotics. She transferred from her

WHAT CAN COMPUTER
VISION DO FOR
NEUROSCIENCE

local college to MIT, declaring a major in Space and Field Robotics, but her real passion was personal companion robots. She continued on to get her Ph.D., working tirelessly on her projects. Then, right around the same time that her pet cat prototype was ready for field testing, she met Karl. Well, she had already known him, since he was a colleague. Karl was a large German man, with a full beard and sensitive eyes.

One day in the lab, he snuck up behind her and uncharacteristically covered her eyes for an oddly timed game of guess who. Annoyed, Martha quickly turned around to face her assailant, only to be lost for a brief second in his eyes. Why hadn't she noticed them before? She was so immersed in her work, she hadn't had a social life to speak of. There was the occasional night of awkward drinks after class, but Martha always was the first to excuse herself and retreat to the safety of her apartment, which was littered with electronics. You would never guess that a woman lived there. Ever since her Aunt Sadie had died, she no longer had anyone reminding her of her duty to show herself out in public. Rarely did she do anything more with her hair than pull it back off of her face, and never did she wear makeup. She didn't even own any, unless you count ChapStick. She was regretting that at this moment. She wondered what Karl's angle was. She was still wondering this after waking up the next morning in his apartment, unclothed and hungover. Karl was an attentive lover, and he accepted Martha just as she was, unibrow and all.

Their courtship was a quick one. They saw no reason to plan a big ceremony, since Martha had no family and Karl's was over in Berlin. They moved into his apartment and immediately started working on adding to their family. Martha was taken by surprise by how powerful her maternal instincts were, since they had laid dormant all of her life. She did worry she would parent like her mother, and was secretly afraid of that. But she trusted in Karl, and with his love and support she decided to take the plunge into motherhood. Sadly, conception did not prove as easy to her as did reading schematics. Every few months or so, she would be met with disappointment as one pregnancy test after another came back negative. She began to feel like a failure as a woman. Karl didn't seem to mind, and held out hope that they would conceive eventually. Which is indeed what happened.

After two years of trying, they welcomed a baby girl that they named Isadora into the world. She was as lovely as a rose bud. Martha relished her role as mother, and all but forgot about her passion for robots. For the first two months of Isadora's life, Martha was completely and blissfully happy. Karl was so proud of his family. Martha loved seeing his gentle eyes shine with love when he held his daughter. He spoke of how his family back in Berlin would be planning a trip to the US soon to finally meet the family. Martha couldn't wait. Then it began.

First it was a night of screaming inconsolably followed by weekly visits to the pediatrician where she was assured that these fits of screaming would pass, and nothing was wrong with Isadora.

Karl was at work and Martha was home with Isadora, trying to find ways to calm the child. She tried rocking her, driving around with her, playing Mozart, but nothing worked. Isadora went through phases of screaming which were only interrupted by brief periods of exhausted and fitful sleep. Martha was becoming unnerved, and decided to try and let Isadora cry it out, so Martha herself could get some rest. She lay Isadora in her crib, closed the door and went in the workshop, where her cat robot looked at her quizzically.

She picked it up and turned it on. It started humming (she was still working on getting the meow sound just right when she and Karl began their relationship) and its head turned from side to side. She began working on her project, wondering how she had gone so long neglecting little Felix. Of course she named him Felix. "Felix the cat, the wonderful, wonderful cat" she remembered these lyrics from a long since forgotten cartoon her Aunt Sadie had watched occasionally. She welcomed the feeling of wires and tools in her hands again, and vowed to finish this project. Suddenly, she started. The clock could not be right! How had five hours passed so quickly; she felt like it had been only thirty minutes.

That's when she heard it. The silence. The cold, foreboding silence. She felt it emanating from Isadora's room and dreaded opening the door. She wondered, for a brief moment if the infant might be asleep. She knew that was not the case, but tried to force herself to believe it as she ascended the stairs to Isadora's room.

She put her ear to the door, to see if she could hear anything. Still nothing. She inhaled deeply and turned the knob. She approached the crib slowly, afraid to rouse the sleeping baby. Isadora lay there still. Her little eyes were wide open, but as empty as her father's were kind. A tinge of blue had already begun to creep into her face. Martha scooped her up and drove to the emergency room as fast as she could. She hadn't bothered to put Isadora in the car seat, but held her close to her with one hand and steered with the other. She ran into the E.R. screaming for help. The nurse came out and escorted her back into the triage room. It was too late; Isadora had been dead for a few hours.

Martha passed out and had to be revived. She had no idea who contacted Karl, but somehow he had found his way to her side.

"What happened?" he asked her, as he held her in his arms. The police had already been questioning her for hours at this point, and the good folks at CPS had interviewed her as well. She could not face those eyes. Those eyes that had once melted her heart, those eyes that believed there was something special about Martha. Those eyes that looked at her very differently now, with suspicion. Martha was racked with guilt. No charges were filed, it was ruled a case of Sudden Infant Death Syndrome.

For a time, Martha and Karl tried to go on. The suggestion to try again for another child was met with disdain and disgust. Martha was not the same person she had been. It upset Karl to see his wife sink deeper and deeper into depression. He spared no expense to try and get her professional help. She still awoke screaming from nightmares, "Isadora? Isadora? Is that you?" only to be met with the cold, empty three am air. She wasn't there. She would never be there. She would never grow up, and Martha just could not accept that. She became increasingly distant from Karl, and it did not surprise her in the least when Karl announced that he had "met someone" at work and would be moving out in a month or so. He promised financial support, but Martha was not concerned. She barely noticed he was even talking to her when he broke the news.

Martha now reclines on her tattered chaise, the once vibrant embroidered lilacs mocking her sagging, pasty body. Alcoholism and certainly many other undiagnosed illnesses (Diabetes) had destroyed her physically as the death of her daughter had done to her mentally. She had moved the chaise into the workshop, so she could comfortably work on her cat robot. She had found a way to create a holographic face on the cat and gave it the ability to move and behave like a real cat. In the past thirty years, she had made dozens of these cats. She kept them in Isadora's old cradle, which to her seemed strangely fitting. Walking up the stairs to the kitchen, she passed a mirror and stopped for some reason. Who was that woman in her house? She looked at herself in the mirror and saw her mother.

She began to smash the mirror with her fist until it broke and she remembered her German husband, Karl and the shattered mirror made her think of Kristallnacht, the night of broken glass. She laughed at this memory and smiled in spite of herself. She was very drunk. She hadn't thought of Karl for years. She went into the kitchen and poured herself another vodka. She stumbled back to her workshop and passed out on the chaise. She awoke to the sound of a dozen robot cats wearing Isadora's face, mewing like newborns and nuzzling her from her stupor, like she had done every morning for the last fifteen years.

Thread

Heidi Andrea Restrepo Rhodes

She held on by a string. A wiry dilapidated red thread that had woven for years between the meanderings, the rush of her legs flying across dreams, the perspirations of survival that had tossed her around like the quick flits of a breaking cello song. A delicate thread that did not waver, tying her to the vast open sky filled with the voices of ghosts, whispers, screams, tender wailing, soft giggles, from the rafters of clouds: she was bound to centuries that welted her skin, the hives of genocides, broken blisters of languages flailing like pus-filled children drowning in the coercions of equatorial plunders.

She hated mirrors. Her gaze evoked breaking glass with every glance, as though the shame of melted sand were weeping for her and could not hold the assemblage of her selves in the tiny frame of one face. History weighed too much for anything hanging on the wall, the call to mimicry too heavy in the face of a thousand faces. The thread had stretched across the sharp shards, dragging splinters into its fibers, to carry the impossibility of replication along with it: a constant reminder that even in the company of her selves, she was isolated, married to her residency on an island of her own. She walked among dogs, among raisin-skinned women and their daughters, in elaborate fur coats, tripping over her own thread as it caught on the tips of their heels while they crooned over macaroons and handsome prospects on their way from tea. (She hated tea. It tasted like Cheshire dirt, elusive bitter nothingness. Like everything else, bland and biting at once, and prone to presenting an illusory quality she could not stand on with two feet.)

The whole world turned around her and all the stillness she slept away beneath the blue of winters, always at the edge, sometimes wrapped in her thread, to stay warm in the fabric of her want, the endless pool of questions and maybes and what-ifs that pervaded her slumber on the darkest of nights.

The thread cut her, strangled her neckline in the suffocating airs of the untenable present, the stark and horrific glow of famines, mass evictions,

the abuse of utilitarian factories. The thread tied her together when she thought her limbs might simply just fall away. It was a tightrope she walked. It was a leash that kept her at bay when she beasted into the crowds like a wolverine in boots. She'd knit it into her every day like an old friend she knew was a detriment to her solvency, but without whom she faired weak, and at times, excessively unhinged. Her melancholy contained her. The thread held her like a kite, securing her from the bluster of her heartbreak and the traumas of a thousand years, midnight hurricanes that felled the ancient trees and the things they knew.

But this she knew: she was not an isolated event. She was not entirely peculiar, nor singular. There were others who like her, felt stuck in the cart-tray, in the nauseating rotations of the world's largest Ferris wheel, her vision blurred towards the axis from which the spinning coerced her movements, her flying.

But is it still called flying if the bird is brigged and tossed through the air?

It was no mistake that her thread, still red in its muddied strain, had tangled itself in the spokes of the wheel, growing tighter and tighter at the pull of her, mangling flesh knots, tattooing pain, scarring her weathered cinnamon skin.

The Ferris wheel was a world speaking worlds, turning and turning like a silent demon costumed in the joy-clothes of a hegemonic fantasy, inventions of bourgeois pleasure, and she recoiled from its hypnosis. It was the maniacal whip of poverty rushing her to the mechanical and tedious bliss, the grip of promises, picket fences, belonging, the semblance of happy. She spun at the center of this carnival, a biting and bitter faith weaving its way into the capillaries of the fair-goers as they sipped something sweet and smug, sinking their lips into sugar-dipped chimeras of an empire on the brink of an unfastening.

And the Ferris wheel turned and turned and turned and turned. And the people laughed and trilled their thrill into the open and wondrous sky with a myopia that left them starless. It was at the top she could breathe, for a moment, before swinging back down again into the thunderous chatter of the multitudes. At the top, where she paused, to take in the night, to gaze upward and recount the mythologies of ages to herself, to whisper a prayer to the lands of her making. From there, she could inspect the panorama of provinces, the profusion of threads interlaced for miles, tying others to the mandates of their domains, and all the dissatisfactions of a public artifice. At the top, she thought, was the territory of gods, the grasp of epochal insights.

She harnessed her courage to view the vast spectacle. To the east, there were massacres, chemical violations, suicides by pencil, or by hanging in the stench of overcrowded mills. To the south, there was pillaging and the death of mothers fending for their histories. To the north, impossible libraries housing the tales of what the world had become and how. And the west, replete with mediocre kings fattening off the desserts of their exploitations, schools for propriety, the rancorous hatred of alterity, the veneration of dazzle, and slaveries manufactured in the guise of participation. And strings, countless strings, tying it all together, piece by piece. Strands of once-upon-a-time crossing over strands of regret. Resentment twining resiliency. Threads of solipsism maneuvering through webs of greed and gain. Children reaching for butterflies. Bindings displaying their exertions, forces like light on water, ethics. Yarns suspending the hunger-animal of barren lands, tacking the unhomedness of exile to innumerable feet. And chains. So many chains. The mapping of anguish.

At the top, she stood, managing to balance the rolling undulations of the floor beneath her as it rocked so very high up in the atmosphere, and opening her eyes to the bright light of the moon, she leapt, unafraid of the arms of the night, and the thread, raveled in an awful tangle, grew tight against her vault, snapping loose from her bones and all the weathering of her years. She fell and fell and fell. She flew and flew and flew. The cello song broke against the ceiling of firmament, perforating the mayhem of complacencies shadowed in the soil of the earth below her. The centuries cocooned her from the dizziness of heights. And there, on the horizon, the gleam of the sun edging forth, emerging another day.

An Obedient Girl

Amy Bridges

"Now, none of us knows what to expect from Mavis Wilkerson," my mother said, looking back in my direction from her position in the front passenger seat.

Several white sheets fluttered in the wind, hanging loosely to clotheslines. I'd started counting them a ways back, as my father drove us, winding in-and-out through back country-roads.

In those days, I often found myself sitting in the backseat of my parents' white Oldsmobile, driven from one supper to the next across the expanse of the Texas Panhandle. The trip to the Wilkerson farm was no different.

At nine-years of age, I was a plump pastor's child who took pride in comprehending that to cut a brisket correctly, one must cut the meat on a bias, lest it be too tough. To reduce the bitterness in collard greens, one must soak the greens in vinegar for at least an hour prior to cooking. For a bowl of sweet turnips, always choose turnips with unblemished skin that are heavy and firm to the touch.

"I've never met a lobotomy survivor before. Have you Charles?" my mother continued.

"I've never met a lobotomy survivor," my Dad answered.

My father was known as Brother Charles to most of the flocks he shepherded in Southern Baptist churches throughout Texas.

He and my mother, LaVon, married young, becoming missionaries in the Middle East, spending years in Beirut and Sidon, which they both preferred to small Texas towns.

One of my mother's favorite stories was relating the drive to catch the plane to Lebanon from LaGuardia in 1969; they passed Woodstock rocking in full swing and didn't pull over.

"We didn't have time for that nonsense. We had plans," she always said. "We wanted to save the world, not get drunk and roll around on it."

My mother fell in love with the Middle East, purchasing a gold-threaded Bedouin bridal dress that she would wear to women's luncheons. She would stand before a rapt group of Texas women, speak Arabic, and feed them all hummus, a food that at the time, could be found nowhere in Texas. My parents left Lebanon when the Civil War started with a promise to return, but as the years passed, it seemed less likely they would ever go back.

"I loved Lebanon," my mother would say. "Americans think Middle Eastern women are quiet and submissive, cloistered up. Nothing could be further from the truth. They might wear the hijab, but that means nothing. It's about modesty. A Middle Eastern woman runs her own home. Most of them have Master's degrees. Many are doctors. All of them have strong opinions and they don't apologize."

My mother embraced everything about Middle Eastern culture except the Holy Prophet Muhammad. She would drink Jasmine tea and sometimes cry longing for a return trip.

"Texas bores the hell out of me," she would say. "I was once held at gun point at a post office in Syria. I once stopped traffic walking down the street in Beirut in high heels. Now it's all chicken fried steak and prayer meetings."

This is one reason I think she was looking forward to the luncheon with Mavis.

"I'm excited about meeting her, though also a little scared," My mother told my father that day in the car. "James never brings her to church."

"James is a strange man. He's always loitering around there, even when he doesn't have to be. It's weird."

"Listen to you. You're the preacher. No one loiters around there more than you. James and Mavis don't have any children. They're on up in years. Maybe he's lonely. How much friendship can you get from a lobotomy survivor?"

"We're about to find out," my Dad said. "We will eat and leave."

"What are they cooking?" I asked, ready for the whole thing to be over with.

"Does it matter?"

"I just want to know what I have to be prepared for. It's one thing to meet crazy people. It's another thing to eat their cooking."

My Dad laughed.

"Stop encouraging her smart mouth," my mother told him.

My mother was adamant that we were to eat whatever we were given, and offend no one in the process. Otherwise, it might misrepresent the message of Christ, which was I guess, "Eat everything."

In truth, I couldn't have been more surprised by Mavis Wilkerson. She was a pleasant woman with a vacant stare. She welcomed us into their home, a large farmhouse, mostly decorated in white with large hand crocheted afghans draped around things that gave it a cozy quality.

"Glad to have you," Mavis said, welcoming us into the dining room, set with china.

My eyes rested immediately on the honey-glazed ham, surrounded by hot sweet potatoes in the center of the table, and I breathed a sigh of relief. Her lobotomy hadn't stopped her from cooking like a sane-minded southerner.

"Glad to have you here, Preacher," James said, taking the head seat at the table. James was an older gentleman of around sixty-five, but was strong and husky. He was clean-shaven, and dressed in a fine suit. He stretched his arm over to Mavis and gave her a squeeze on the shoulders. "Mavis here cooked this whole meal herself. Didn't give her a bit of help. She's a good cook, this one. Think I might have to keep her."

Mavis didn't respond to his touch, other than to keep the same smile, and the same look ahead of her.

"James loves my cooking," she said pleasantly.

"You're a fine cook, Mavis," he told her. "You do things perfect without a complaint."

It was an odd thing to say. But Mavis looked toward James, and he at her, sharing a small moment that could've been a tender one.

Then Mavis began serving up the food.

"This is quite a spread," my mother told her. "These creamed potatoes look delicious."

"They're James' favorite," Mavis answered. "Bacon bits. Sour Cream. Pepper. Buuuu…" and her voice trailed off. She stared ahead like she'd been entranced by some invisible thing off in the distance.

James put his hand on her shoulder and gave her a little shake. "Butter," he said. "She uses butter."

"Butter," she said, looking back at my mother. "Thank you."

"You went off into Crazy Land again," he said gruffly, as she put ham and potatoes onto his plate.

"I. I have trouble…Staying focused," she said, looking at my mother.

"I know what you mean," my mother answered, trying to lighten the mood. "I often lose track of my thinking."

"Not the way Mavis does," James laughed.

Mavis looked over at James and laughed too.

"Mavis would stare like that for an hour if you didn't give her a little shake now-and-again. A restart. But she sure is cooperative. Wasn't always that way, were you?"

"I had a little bit of a temper," she said. "Depressed."

"Enough of that," James said, cutting her off. "This isn't a therapy session."

Everything was quiet.

"You know what?" my Dad said, breaking the tension. "We haven't blessed this meal."

Though farmers are generally quiet-natured, James talked a blue streak, telling stories about the town, commenting on the weather, even giving a run-down of the church books at one point, listing the tithers.

Mostly, whatever James would say, Mavis would agree with, smiling in a hollow way and wiping her hands on her lap napkin.

I stuffed my face and watched her closely. Something wasn't right with her. Sure, if you were to take her out in public, she could get along okay. She could smile and exchange pleasantries like the rest of us, but if you watched closely, there were cracks. Maybe that was why she never left the house. Maybe that was why he never brought her to church.

When Mavis refilled my potatoes, I thanked her. She looked at me then and said, "You are an obedient child. That is the work of the mother."

She looked at my mom.

"Amy is an obedient girl," Mavis said again, smiling. Then she looked over at James. "Amy is an obedient girl, isn't she, James?"

"She's quiet. She does what she's told. Hardly see that anymore," James answered.

"Thanks," I whispered, and somehow, though Mavis meant it with the best of intentions, it didn't feel at all like a compliment. My stomach was hurting, but I kept eating the potatoes. James was right about Mavis. She was an excellent cook.

Shortly thereafter, my obedience paid off, when Mavis announced, "I made a pie. Special for you, Amy. A lime flavored Refrigerator Pie."

Mavis saw the delight in my eyes.

The Refrigerator Pie was my favorite of all pies. It was a staple among small country potlucks. The pie was never cooked, but cooled in the

refrigerator.

"I'll give you the biggest piece. I'll serve you first."

I was thrilled with Mavis at this point, and could've seen myself heading over there after school in the future for cookies and homework.

James got up from the table, looked at my Dad and said, "I have something to show you, Preacher."

For a moment, I thought I saw a crack in Mavis' demeanor; something that perhaps indicated not all was sunshine and unicorns.

"James doesn't like sweets," she said, handing me the pie. Her hand was shaking. Was it nerves? A side effect of the lobotomy? "I always wanted a daughter."

The thoughts were not connected, but at this point, I didn't care.

The sensation of biting into that pie, the creamy sweetness was euphoric. Though my stomach felt nervous, I couldn't stop eating it. I didn't notice when James re-entered the room. I vaguely remember thinking, 'Is he wearing a choir robe?'

The pie was a beautiful combination of citrus and cream. It was delicate, yet strong. It was put together perfectly, then topped off with a homemade whipped topping that was light airy perfection.

I was brought out suddenly by James' clear and sharp voice. "I've brought you some reading materials, Preacher."

There was a sharp thud at the end of the table. A large stack of about seven Aryan Nation Magazines landed between the half-eaten ham and the silver coffee pot.

There was a moment of silence before my Dad said, "What is this?"

James Wilkerson then reached into the pocket of his long white choir robe, and pulled out a white hood with eye-holes cut out of the front of it, and a pointy top. He pulled it onto his head, making one thing clear to all of us: The tone of the meal had changed. This was no longer a simple luncheon, hosted by a gracious farmer and his lobotomized wife. This was James Wilkerson's coming-out party as a regular member of the KKK.

James Wilkerson stood silently at the head of the table. This was, in fact, the first time he'd been silent through the entirety of the meal.

We all sat in shocked horror unable to eat. Except for Mavis, who continued to enjoy her pie same as before. She wore a kind of ho-hum expression that said, 'Just another day with a six-foot Klansman making threats at the head of the dinner table.'

"You like this pie, don't you, Amy?" Mavis asked me, noticing I'd paused.

"Yes ma'am," I answered.

"Then, have some more," she told me, digging into the pan to serve me another piece. I didn't want anymore. As good as it was, my stomach was turning. I looked at my mother expecting her to put an end to the pie pig-out. But she sat in stone silence with her eyes glued to James.

James raised his right hand, and in a loud voice said, "As Imperial Kleagle, it has come to my attention that you have been bussing Mexicans into Sunday school."

I knew my Dad had been using the church bus to pick up some Latino children for Sunday school. That was true.

But none of us had any idea what an Imperial Kleagle was. It sounded like a Star Wars villain. Since then, we've learned it is the title given to a recruiter for the Ku Klux Klan. Regardless, judging from the background I had of the KKK, and the enraged authority with which James made the statement, I didn't think he was complimenting my father.

"You're right I've been picking them up," my Dad said, "and I'm gonna keep doing it."

The tension in the room made me eat. I could feel my stomach expanding, but I couldn't stop. The pie was addictive.

"I always serve pie with forks," Mavis said, as though it was just the two of us there in the room. "When I used to have electro-shocks, they'd stick spoons in our mouths and instead of screaming we'd bite them. I'd always gag on those spoons so now I don't use them."

"What are electro-shocks?" I asked.

My mother reached her hand over and gave me a pinch on the leg. "Let's go," she said, taking me by the hand and heading fast for the door.

"Ya'll taking off?" Mavis called behind us.

"You're gonna have a problem with us, Brother Charles." James' voice was loud and stern.

"Don't try to intimidate me."

My stomach was turning over, the sour from the lime pie trickling up my throat like hot acid.

I felt my mother's hand.

"Get to the car," she said, shoving me out the front door.

My Dad's voice was behind me, strong and fierce. "You are a coward," he told James. "You need to get yourself right with God."

The pie was hot slime in my throat. It wasn't the delicious creaminess from before. Now it was Mavis' chunky brains erupting from deep inside me. With each step toward the car, it was coming up.

My Dad was behind us when it erupted. My mother's hand pushed me on, the hot green vomit shooting out of me like rivers. The pie was an ugly lake stretching from the front door of the Wilkersons' to the side of the car, then pooling in my lap and the floorboards in the backseat beneath me; all Mavis Wilkerson's hard work coming up in hot and terrible chunks.

The sound as we pulled away from the Wilkersons' was the gravel road, my mother's sobs, and my own retching.

Amy is an obedient girl.

The Refrigerator Pie was a wet and green baptism.

A final image of the Wilkersons' that stays with me: A lovely farmhouse with a strange ghost man shrouded in white. The woman standing next to him has a pleasant expression.

They are both wearing masks.

Litany

Sheila Lamb

Asudden screech of tires stopped at her feet in the post office parking lot. She didn't recognize the driver. He leaned out his pick-up truck window, over the bench seat to the passenger side, the one closest to her face, and he spit his obscenities:

—whore

—slut

—cunt

Then he spit for real. It landed on her left elbow. The truck's hot black tire touched the edge of her left boot, where the outsole extended out from the dusty leather. He drove away, tires squealing upon his exit. The smell of burnt rubber lingered in the summer air. She kept walking. She had to buy stamps.

"Need help?" the postal clerk asked. He'd come to check on her.

Kai shook her head and stopped hitting the machine. Her fist throbbed. She had pounded on the Plexiglas, over and over, until a booklet of stamps fell into the tray. Right then, she was grateful for the clerk. She needed to hear a voice that was clean. She needed clear words to wash away what had been thrown on her—garbage, words from a man she did not know.

She forced herself past the glass doors etched with a white frosted eagle and flag, out into the heat. Those words were not meant for her. She was not those things. Yet she felt as if a layer of fine silt covered her, filled her eyes, clogged her breath. She resisted the urge to go back inside, to the cool damp of the whirring air conditioner, and listen to the clerk in the pale blue uniform speak quietly about brown paper for packages.

She paused at the curb and wiped her sweating palms on her jeans. She looked left and right for wayward trucks. Her stomach lurched as she crossed the heat-softened asphalt back to her own Ford pick-up.

With shaking hands, she turned the steering wheel a hard left away from town.

Kai's trailer home sat off of 89A, past Sunset Crater but before the Babbitt ranch. She could have been living in Tuba City with the rest of her family. But she told them she preferred this place - the cleanness of the high desert. No traffic, no noise, no alcohol.

Almost everyone she'd known drank too much, her mother and father included. Kai had decided at a young age that she didn't want to be tainted by the drink. She'd seen her older brother puking into toilets. Her sister was now wheelchair bound. She'd been mangled after an accident where her drunken boyfriend's car had suspended precariously close to the edge of the Cameron Bridge. Her sister had been thrown onto the pavement. She survived. The boyfriend and the car did not.

Kai rented five acres of her uncle's trust land, a lengthy sliver. She had taken her old horse, Dancer. Soon, she'd buy another horse. Start a ranch. She thought if she could get the horse ranch going, her uncle might let her lease more of his property. Kai could have leased land from other relatives, but her uncle's property appealed to her. It edged along a national monument site of ancient pueblos built by ancient ancestors. There was an argument as to who really built the orange brick walls. Anasazi, Sinaguans, Hopi, but not Navajo. Not Diné.

On trips to visit her uncle, her parents would drive past the clay brick ruins. She'd press her face against the car window, wanting to touch the brick. Longing. She shouldn't touch the pueblos, her uncle had warned. She shouldn't go near them. Disturbing the interior of Anasazi homes could bring bad luck. Or worse.

But she was not traditional. Raised Christian, she'd gone to church every Sunday. Now, with classes and work, she went only on holidays with her parents. Kai didn't believe the old stories of bad luck and disturbing spirits. Not really. Things happened, either way.

Kai waited until darkness fell. The cold desert air rose around her, seeping upwards, laced with the dry scent of sage and rabbit brush. She hiked in the silent twilight to Lomaki, one of the ruins tucked into an isolated bluff. The four crumbling walls and no roof protected her more than her trailer. She found it hard to explain why she was attracted to the old pueblos. Not that anyone asked. Not that she ever had to explain.

She took nothing. No light. No candle. She sat. She looked up at the stars.

—whore

—slut

—cunt

The stars shone down.

He did not know her. She did not know him. A horrible stream of words connected them. In the cool desert dark, she would break it. If she was the only one to hear it, then she could also forget. Erase it. The screeched stop of the truck, the black mark on the edge of her boot, did not exist. Break the litany that bound them together, even in memory. She would forget. She would be scrubbed clean as the high desert oaks. She would be free of that echo.

The next day, she rode Dancer across her uncle's trust land and beyond. She strayed through the patchwork of various families' property. As long as she didn't obviously trespass on the Babbitt ranch or the main roads of the national park, she could ride where she chose.

As she rode Dancer eastward, Kai waved to Ana Yazzie. Ana walked in her elderly, bent way to let her churro sheep out to pasture. Sometimes Kai saw Clint Yazzie on his way to his hogan, where he would spend his days trying to heal his lame leg. Kai suspected he went out there to sit and wait for death to end his pain.

She wanted to tell him about Lomaki. That would heal him, beneath the pure starlight in the cold night. But she always held back. He wouldn't go inside that pueblo. A traditional Navajo, he'd be terrified. No amount of cleansing ritual would make the pueblo safe for him. It didn't matter. Lomaki, hidden in the hillside, rarely visited by tourists, was hers.

She pulled Dancer's reigns to a halt. The wash that separated Navajo land from the park was rutted, filled with beer cans and pornographic magazines. It's where the boys drank. Looked at dirty pictures. Hot wind blew back one of the pages. A naked man, a white man but he wasn't white. His skin was tanned, darker than hers. He knelt behind a naked blond woman, who was on her hands and knees. Like a dog. Like an animal. Her oversized breasts hung down like cantaloupes.

—whore

—slut

—cunt

She tugged at Dancer's reigns. They turned back. The glossy paper

images clung to Dancer's hooves.

Once, she had been with Benji Begay. It was the summer after she moved to her trailer. Her first move of independence. They'd been bookish friends at Tuba City High School, the few who didn't sneak their parents' beer at graduation parties. Being with Benji was an experiment, purposely ignoring her Baptist upbringing, to see how it felt. Sex was awkward. Fumbling. But she understood the potential. When he held her for a few minutes afterwards, she felt warm. Safe. She wanted Benji to return so they could try it again. He had said he would call. That was two years ago.

Sunset. She visited the main pueblo of the park when the tourists had gone. Downhill from the buildings was a circular structure, a ball court. In the center of the ancient ball court was a smooth depression. Tadpoles floated atop the red sandstone. Kai watched them flit underneath the surface of the rainwater puddle.

Tiny waves appeared in the water as the tadpoles flashed back and forth in the last rays of sun. She wondered if they would survive, what planted them there. Each day, the sun would rise, gain heat, and evaporate the water. Then monsoon rains created the puddle anew.

Dissolve. Disperse. Back to the clouds, rising upward and where do the tadpoles go?

The following weekend was the Babbitt Ranch auction. She'd saved her money, sold a harness, an old saddle. She went to see how it worked, to meet her neighbors. Networking was what her occasional business classes at the college promoted. She wasn't interested in the Internet. It wouldn't connect at her mobile home anyhow. But she could talk to people about horses. The idea of socializing didn't appeal to her either but she knew she couldn't start a business all by herself. And, if she was lucky, she might be able to invest in one new horse.

The jostling of the crowd took some getting used to. She spent most of the morning in the stands, observing, with her uncle. He'd agreed to meet her. He'd introduce her to the nearby ranchers. Maybe they'd let her apprentice with them. Work for a summer or two until she learned the ropes. She watched how the cowboys handled the animals, which horses got the highest bids. She discovered, happily, that her intuition on price and quality were correct.

"Look here." Her uncle pointed out the structure and cut of muscle across the horse's hindquarters. "This is a strong horse. She just needs a little TLC, good feeding, good shelter. She'll breed well if that's what you want."

Kai thought she might take the chance on the skinny chestnut sorrel filly. The bids were low and few, and after the third round, the animal was hers. A small thrill went through her. Her first purchase. The first step toward her dream.

She led the filly to her truck, horse trailer hitched and ready. Then she stopped cold and the animal halted; the horse's warm breath blew a question mark in her ear.

The man who had said those horrible things in the post office parking lot sat on her bale of timothy hay. She had tried to excise him from her life. But there he was, sitting on her stack of feed, leaning against her back truck tire. The cold Lomaki stars settled in her gut.

"I need that." She wrapped her shaking hands tightly in the horse's reigns.

He had a sun-colored beard and he wore flannel, his shirt rolled up at the sleeves. It was too hot for flannel and beards. He squinted in the brightness then pulled down the brim of his beat-up hat.

"What? You need help moving this?" He nodded down toward the timothy.

Her long black hair was kept in place by her own cowboy hat. She didn't like that similarity despite the fact that every person at the auction wore a hat. Her black eyes trained on his. She wondered if he was a coyote trick.

"What do you need, lady?" He stood and lifted the bale by the twine. "Here. You want me to put this somewhere for you?"

He dropped it into the bed of her yellow pick up. She walked the horse around the far side of the truck toward the hitched trailer. She kept her distance from the man. He didn't seem to recognize her. She tried to reconcile the gruff, somewhat helpful cowboy with the man who had yelled at her, spit on her.

She could pretend it didn't happen. Say nothing to him and go on her way. Or she could let him know what he had done. To use her voice for herself.

"I saw you. The other day. At the post office."

He glanced at her again before he tugged on his hat. Pulled the brim over his eyes. Looked to the ground. "I thought you was someone else."

"I wasn't someone else." She'd spoken. Made him recognize her. How little it fulfilled her.

Kai broke her gaze from him and turned her attention to the horse. She whispered to the filly, stroked her nose gently, encouraging her onto the metal ramp. The horse nickered and whinnied. It took a while to coax the animal in, one clanging step at a time. Inside the trailer was dim and hot. Kai was glad for the protective metal walls. A shield. She hoped that if she took long enough, the man would be gone. She heard his boot scraping the ground. He kicked dirt. The horse was settled, her water trough filled. Kai couldn't stay inside there forever. She walked out against the sun.

He talked to her over the bed of the truck. "Look. I didn't mean it to be for you. I don't even know you."

"You meant it to be for someone." She dug her keys from her pocket. She wanted to leave. She wanted him to be gone.

"That girl told lies about me."

"So?" What girl? His reasons didn't matter to her. She didn't want to know anything about him.

"Look, I just apologized. Okay?" He slapped his hat against his thighs. His blond hair stayed plastered and wet against his head. "I'm trying here. Trying to tell you I made a mistake. I thought you was someone else, is all." He circled in the dust and jabbed his booted toe into her truck tire. "Anyway. I've been here trying to find a job."

He shrugged. Conversational. Like his apology would make it all okay.

The filly stomped, impatient within her confines. Kai thought about the time it would take to break her. She'd signed up for another business class at the university. And one of the Babbitt hands had offered her a job of helping to close down the auction. No pay but she couldn't pass up the experience.

This man could help her, if he really needed work. He could break the new horse while she went to class. She wouldn't be able to pay him. Room and board? No, her spare room would remain empty. She could offer a campsite somewhere on her land. She could, if he were someone else.

"Goddamn. Are you going to say anything?" He kicked at the tire again. "I'm just trying to say I made a mistake."

The words. In her mind. His voice.

—whore

—slut

—cunt

"Can't you accept an apology?" He twisted his hat. She thought that if he were a dog, he'd be begging for scraps.

She checked the latches on the ramp, and then with a full swing, shut the gate.

"No."

She stabled the new filly in the stall next to Dancer. Her mind replayed her conversation with the man, a continuous loop. Strength threaded up her spine. Yet the words were there, unchanged. Terror struck her and the short-lived tingle of strength disappeared. His voice would never go away. She'd always hear that echo in her mind. She breathed deep, inhaling the warm scent of her horses and the sharpness of grassy hay. She was supposed to forgive. Let go. Childhood Sunday school lessons. Simplistic phrases that left her empty.

Dusk commenced. She ran to the pueblo. But not Lomaki. The words seemed to hang above the roofless bricks, like wisps of smoke from a cold fire.

Across the cinder path from the ball court was the blowhole, a geological mystery. The federal government placed a grate over the opening. The park rangers couldn't be responsible for someone falling in. Some days, the air from the hole in the ground blew outward. Other days, air was sucked into the earth, by some unknown force of geophysics. On those days, she feared if she opened her mouth near it, her very soul would be sucked out, down. Even though she didn't believe in it, she whispered a silent prayer of protection.

Kai lay flat on the ground, her face pressed against the black steel bars. The coldness blew out of the earth, toward the blue sky. It made her head ache but she remained. The constant force of crater air enveloped her face, an internal coldness borne in the dark core. She opened her mouth against the rush of outward air and hoped soul could be blown in.

Contributors

Farah Ahamed grew up in Nairobi and now works in London. She has almost completed the University of East Anglia's Advanced Creative Writing Diploma under the guidance of Louise Doughty. Her short stories have been published by *Kwani?*, Fey Publishing, Bridge House Publishers and Fringeworks. In March 2014, her short story was nominated by *Kwani?* for the Caine Prize for African Writing and she was also selected for a mentorship programme with novelist Courttia Newland. She is Digital Writer in Residence at the Mary Ward Centre in London; her blog which encourages debate and engagement in women and the arts can be found at This Woman's Work 2014 (http://thiswomanswork2014.tumblr.com/writer).

Henri Bensussen has published poems and stories in various journals and anthologies, including *Blue Mesa Review*, *Eclipse*, *Skin to Skin*, and *Common Ground Review*. She serves on the board of the Mendocino Coast Writers Conference, and otherwise collects plants, bird lists, discarded metal objects of no known use, and anything that can be added to a compost pile, a story, or a poem; she herself is decomposing in the dews and fogs of coastal living.

Amy Bridges is a writer whose work has appeared on TLC, HGTV, and Discovery Health. She is a Hedgebrook alumna, and the recipient of the First Prize Fiction Award at the San Francisco Writers Conference. Her play, *Women of the Holocaust*, was published by The Kennedy Center and *The Northwest Theatre Journal*. Her play, *The Day Maggie Blew Off Her Head*, received first prize in the Edward Albee Prince William Sound Playwriting Lab, presented by Edward Albee. Her work has been nominated for The American Theatre Critics Association's New Play Award as well as The Osborne Award for an Emerging Playwright. Currently, she is working on a novel. And of course, living in Hollywood, it is required for her to always be working on a screenplay.

Leah Chaffins is currently working on her MFA at Oklahoma City University. She has short stories and news articles published in *The Cameron Goldmine, The Red Earth Review, The Cameron Collegian, Cliterature* and *Okie Mag.* Chaffins has worked as an editor for both the *Goldmine* and for *CyberSoliel Fine Arts Journal.* She also is a university English Instructor where she hopes to share the joy of writing with others.Chaffins writes mostly short horror stories, and memoir. She is nearing completion of her first novel, and the completion of two short story compilations, *Gravel Goats,* which are memoirs, and *Reflecting an Eidola,* short horror stories.

R. Crawford studies English Literature and Comparative Literature at the University of Rochester, and is a TA for Russian Drama. She has interned with Open Letter, literary translation press at the University of Rochester. She has been awarded the Book Awards in Comparative Literature. Rachel has been a part of the literary community in Rochester, NY including volunteering to organize the American Literary Translation Conference in 2012.

Judith Day grew up in St. Louis and began writing fiction at age five, as a way to stay sane. She now lives sanely and happily with her husband in northern California and is still writing fiction. She has been a psychotherapist for 28 years and is currently working with military service members and their families.

Gabriela Denise Frank is a Detroit native and Seattle resident, and is the author of *CivitaVeritas: An Italian Fellowship Journey,* published in 2011. The book documents her experience living in the unique Italian hilltown of Civita di Bagnoregio while on a fellowship sponsored by the Northwest Institute for Architecture and Urban Studies in Italy. The following year, she was selected to participate in the Jack Straw Writers Program, which introduces Northwest writers to the medium of recorded audio and encourages the creation of new literary works.

A 2013 graduate of Artist Trust's EDGE Development Program for Literary Artists, Gabriela's work has appeared in a variety of publications including *ARCADE, Seattle Daily Journal of Commerce, Forum,* and *Trim Tab.* Her weekly blog, *Hidden City Diaries: Essays from Life,* can be found at gabrieladenisefrank.com.

Laura Hartenberger's writing has appeared or is forthcoming in *The Massachusetts Review, Cutbank Magazine, Dragnet, Winter Tangerine Review, NANO Fiction, Found Poetry Review* and other journals, and has won prizes from *Gulf Coast Magazine* and *The Hart House Review.* She lives in Toronto.

Sheila Lamb received an MFA from Queens University of Charlotte and an M.Ed. in Curriculum and Instruction from George Mason University. Her writing has appeared in *Monkeybicycle, JMWW, The Westchester Review,* and elsewhere. Her work has earned Pushcart and storySouth Million Writers Award nominations and she's also the editor for the *Santa Fe Writers Project Journal.* She lives, teaches, and writes in the mountains of Virginia.

Tracie Orsi has owned and operated Ragin' Cajun Restaurant in Belmar, New Jersey since 1992. Her cookbook *Sittin' Bayou Makes Me Hot!* was released in July 2012. She writes for local publications and is involved with Tourism and the local Arts Council. The past four years she has attended Borderlands Press Writer's Bootcamp to hone her skills as a writer. She is currently working on three novels in different genres and has written several short stories. She generally writes dark fiction, but like any good storyteller, she's also good for a lighthearted tale or two. She says, "Life is hard, it's meant to be. But it sure can be funny sometimes." She lives in Toms River, New Jersey with her husband Cliff, their white lab Belle, a parrotlet named Kaya, and a few fish in the pond in their backyard.

Vivian Papp lives in White Plains, NY with her husband and 5 children. She spent quite a few years at home raising her children, until one day she decided to take a few classes at her local community college. This endeavor led to her transferring to and graduating from Columbia University with a BA in English Literature and subsequently receiving her MA in British and American Literature from Hunter College. She has been an adjunct professor of English at Pace University and Westchester Community College. Her area of specialty is 18th Century British Satire and Medieval Women Writers. Her academic work has been presented at numerous conferences and she is currently working on a science fiction novel and on her PhD in Restoration and 18th Century British Literature at Fordham University. In her spare time, she enjoys collecting antique books and watching action films.

Loreal Prystaj is a visual artist based in New York City. She was born and raised upstate in Rochester and has always loved visually creating: from illustrating and sculpting to painting and photography. Her work is eye catching, full of movement, vibrant color, and is playful to all stretches of the imagination, with, at times, a dark twist. Loreal has spoken at accredited universities, such as NYU and The Fashion Institute of Technology. Her work has been shown in exhibits in California, Vermont, upstate New York, and Manhattan. This past summer her work was exhibited in Pinyoa, China, at the Pinyoa Art Exhibit. Presently she has a collaborative installation piece in New York City's Soho district and her work is part of the permanent collection of the Erie Art Museum in Pennsylvania. She has been published in *CREEM Magazine*, *Icon*, *Niche*, and *ArtBuzz*. Loreal continues to express her ideas through the eye of the lens, and grows as an artist. She and her work are inspirational, complex, often simple, and continues to expand.

Colleen Quinn grew up in upstate New York and was educated at Syracuse University. Her short fiction has appeared in *Spinetingler Magazine*, *The Brooklyn Rail*, and *Gemini Magazine*. She currently resides in Brooklyn, NY, where she works in the advertising industry.

Heidi Andrea Restrepo Rhodes is a Queer, Brown/Colombian/Latina, poet, writer, scholar, artist, and political activist. Her performance, creative writing, and photography have been seen in places such as San Francisco's SomArts, Galería de la Raza, the SICK Collective, the *Mixed Race Queer and Feminist Zine*, Brown and Proud Press, *Codex*, *Wilde*, the *Blue Lyra Review*, and others. She also has some writing being published in a forthcoming anthology on sexual violence, as well as in *The Progressive*, *Mobius*, and *From the Ground Up*. She is currently co-editor of *Reveries and Rage*, an anthology in-progress, which will feature work by Queer and Transgender Writers of Color. She also has an independent photography and oral history project underway, entitled 'The Treacherous Felicity in Relentless Dissent.' Heidi Andrea has an M.A. in a social justice-based Anthropology, and currently lives in Brooklyn.

P.J. Schaefer earned her Ph.D. in American literature at Fordham University, New York and teaches at SUNY Westchester Community College. She is a published freelance writer and editor of long and short mainstream fiction and nonfiction, and her works have appeared in such publications as *Troika, Dogsongs, Elements, Ink., Poor Katie's Almanac, Offshore: Northeast Boating, Boston Parents' Paper, Big Apple Parent, Children's Writer, Family Times, Naturally Women Magazine,* and *Camping Today*. Her academic publications include essays for *The Western Journal of Black Studies, The Journal of Black Studies, A.T.Q.: 19th Century American Literature and Culture, The Facts on File Companion to the American Short Story, Literary Themes for Students: War and Peace, The Facts on File Companion to the American Novel,* and *Teaching English in the Two-Year College.*

Nikki Vogel lives in Edmonton, Alberta, Canada. She was recently awarded an MFA Creative Writing from UBC. In addition to seeking a publishing house for the collection of short stories that comprised her thesis project, Nikki is currently revising a YA novel. When her muse allows her to step away from the computer she plays tennis, cycles and reads voraciously from all genres.

Rose Yndigoyen is a freelance writer and archivist in New York City. She has written for the websites AfterEllen and Biographile and examines queer and feminist issues in pop culture on her blog, The Ladyist. She is a co-creator and co-host of the podcast Pretty Little Recaps. Rose was a 2013 Lambda Literary fellow, and is hard at work on her first novel, a queer young adult love story. Rose lives with her wife in northern Manhattan. They are proud foster parents.

About NLSP

We are New Lit Salon Press and we create books. We are writers. We are artists. We are makers with a mission: to publish the best and brightest, to amplify the voice of a generation lost in the void of a system concerned only about million dollar bestsellers. We look to the past but move boldly towards the future.

Founded by Brian Centrone (Publisher) and Jordan M. Scoggins (Creative Director) in 2012, New Lit Salon Press is based on the principle that Words and Art can and should coexist. NLSP is committed to publishing essays, stories, poems, novels, and art from undiscovered writers and promising artists who struggle to thrive in a marketplace that fails to recognize their talent. We believe in what you do.

The world of publishing is changing. NLSP not only recognises that but embraces it. To meet the demands of the evolving marketplace, NLSP releases are available on all major ebook platforms. However, because we are suckers for the printed page and we love the artistry of a physical object, we have teamed up with bd-studios.com to produce special, luxe print-on-demand editions of select titles.

With over 20 collective years of experience in creative, publishing, technology, and academic fields, we bring a unique skill set to the table. Our comprehensive approach is designed to nurture new and unheard talent in ways most indie publishers do not. We love what we do (and hope you do too).

We are artists. We are writers. We are NLSP and we create books.